Where Else

Else

Turnabout Volume I

RUSS WOOD

DEDICATION

To Brandon and Amber:
Myoki-Achiaba

IMPORTANT AUTHOR'S NOTE

This book is comprised of two separate but connected stories. You may start with either story and then flip the book over and read the other. Depending on which side you start on, the title is either *Where Else*, or *Elsewhere*. Your experience with the stories might differ from someone who has read it in the opposite order.

So make your choice…

1

Armageddon came by way of Meteorite.

While the people of Earth were putting all their resources into combating climate change and terrorism, the real threat came from outside. The meteorite was spotted and touched down within a month's time. There was no preparing. Some even hoped it would miss. The world's leaders launched missiles at it, but that only made the rain of destruction more terrible.

The skies were darkened, crops and people died by the masses, and the planet was thrown off its orbit ever so slightly. But it was enough to put a fixed end date to all life that previously thrived 92,960,000 miles from the sun. One year, maybe less. Earth erupted into chaos. Some abandoned conventions of morality in the face of certain destruction and did whatever they pleased, others gathered and prayed to whatever deity they believed could deliver them, but those with means set about looking for a way to survive.

There was a scramble for solutions: The brightest minds were brought together in hopes they could find a solution and ensure their survival. The leading aerospace engineers, astrophysicists, quantum physics theorists,

geneticists, nutritionists, botanists, biologists and other
scientists came together and decided our fate rested on
traveling to a new home on another planet similar to Earth.

    The NASA Kepler mission was the best hope they
had for finding a habitable planet. Up until the meteorite
struck, the Kepler mission was monitoring a section of stars
in our galaxy most likely to have a similar-sized planet
orbiting at approximately the same distance from its sun as
Earth did to Sol. They did so by measuring the amount of
time the light from the star was dimmed, and how often,
indicating a planet was passing in between the star and Earth
and giving us a vague idea of its size and orbital frequency.
Keppler-186f was believed to be the best chance we had for a
second home. The planet was orbiting in the habitable zone
around star 186, and humanity would cast its last hopes in
this direction.

    The biggest problem was distance. Keppler-186f
(named planet Hope) was 490 light years away, and at the
time, the people of Earth had not figured out how to travel at
the speed of light. Their fastest spacecraft at the time would
take millions of years to cover that distance. Cryogenic
freezing hadn't been invented, neither had anyone been
allowed to experiment with genetically modifying humans to
live longer. But faced with their mortality, the people of
Earth ignored the rules of the Human Rights Commission

and frantically began searching for solutions through the avenue of science. With pharmaceutical corporations no longer holding the reigns of research, quick progress could be made. All solutions were on the table, but it would have to happen "on the fly," literally.

Desperation being their primary motivation, they created the Photon Drive, which harnessed the power of light particles and converted that to physical motion. Travel at the speed of light was now possible, but time limited the testing of genetic modifications in humans to prolong life, as well as cryogenic freezing and reanimation. But those on the voyage would literally have the rest of their lives to figure it out.

They planned to cast off when the Earth's average temperature reached 130 degrees Fahrenheit. To be included on the voyage were people of prestige, power, and means, along with whomever they deemed beneficial to them. A variety of scientists, doctors and engineers bought their tickets with knowledge. Some were compelled to go through force, leaving behind families whose talents were unworthy of the consideration of those in power. Altruism and diversity be damned; this was survival of the fittest.

Ten months after the meteorite struck, they left Earth forever on *The Exodus*.

2

"Rise and shine, son of mine!"

Joshua sat up in his sleeping cubicle and rubbed his eyes. His father sat on the edge of his bunk, holding an open packet of food and a spoon.

"Here's breakfast," he said. Joshua took the packet and began eating. "Are you aware of what day this is?"

Joshua blinked a few times and then answered, "Sleep day."

"Bingo! So we shouldn't waste any more time sleeping, should we?" Joshua laughed at his father's joke, then wiped the food off his chin he had accidentally spat out.

"No, I suppose we shouldn't," Joshua agreed. Then he stopped smiling. "Dad, you said you would tell me about mom someday. I might not wake up, and even if I *do*, you won't be there to tell me then. How's today for 'someday?'"

Tom smiled, but there was hurt in his eyes. He pulled his son's head into his chest and held him close for a second. "Josh, I'm sure you already know the answer to that question by now."

Joshua pulled away, no longer interested in finishing his food. "Yeah, but I still want *you* to tell me."

Tom sighed heavily. "Well, your 'mother' was a mix of whatever genes would eliminate sicknesses and slow down aging."

"So I'm really just a genetic experiment, then. Just like every other kid my age on the ship."

"Not *just* a genetic experiment, Josh. When you put it like that, it feels like you're *trying* to create distance between us."

Joshua looked away, "Maybe that's how I'm coping with saying goodbye to you forever."

Tom gently turned Joshua's head back so he could look him in the eyes. "You're my boy. I raised you. And just because I won't see you again in my lifetime doesn't mean I won't ever see you again."

"If you believed that, why didn't you kill yourself before being taken from your wife and kids on Earth?" Tom sat up straight, wide-eyed.

"Dad, I'm a connector. I see things everyone else misses. You spend hours sometimes on the same page of a book, but you're not looking at the words. You're looking at your bookmark… a photo of a woman and three children posing in front of an Earth geyser. Your family. You were standing behind the camera. It hurts you every day that you were forced to come and they had to be left behind."

Tom looked down at his hands and tried to swallow past the invisible grip around his throat. "I haven't given up hope that God will allow us to be together again. But it's got to be on His time. If I had killed myself, I would have robbed myself of raising you. You are my son, even if you're not *hers*." He looked up with fierceness in his eyes. "The godless 'elites' that brought me here to create your generation thinks physical survival is the only chance they have. I don't!'"

Tom continued: "I know you're a connector. I made you that way. I found the key to unlocking savant-like abilities and made sure to give it to the one child in the Darwin Generation I could guide to use those abilities correctly.

"The first time I noticed you'd connected both hemispheres of your brain was when you were four." Tom reached behind him and pulled a binder out of the cubby. He then removed a colorful drawing from a sheet protector. "Do you remember doing this?"

"Vaguely," Joshua replied as he took the drawing.

"This was your first Mozart drawing. I noticed you were busy scribbling away when I was listening to *The Requiem* one night, and at first I just thought it was random colors and…"

Joshua started humming the lilting melody of *Lacrimosa*.

"You can still read it?" Tom asked.

"Of course. These colors and shapes haven't changed for me."

"See? You connect your logical, verbal hemisphere with your visual one to create connections none of the rest of us can see!" His father demonstrated this by placing his two closed fists together, fingers touching, resembling the two hemispheres of the brain. "Believe it or not, the rest of us don't see words, sounds and numbers as colorful shapes."

"And I'm sure that skill will come in handy when someone wants to translate a song into an ugly drawing," Joshua said.

"Don't sell yourself short. It's not *just* the pictures. You can perform complex calculations in an instant. You learn faster than anyone I've ever known, and then can recall the slightest details. Like the time you put our lab back together *exactly* the way it was a year earlier, after we had to restart our experiment from the beginning."

"Lucky guess," Joshua said.

"And I'm sure the fact that you memorized pi to forty thousand digits in less than an hour didn't have anything to do with your ability to recall minutiae? You said yourself it was just like creating a colorful landscape in your head. That's not how most people memorize numbers!"

"I just did that to pass the time," Joshua replied. "I think *anyone* stuck on this tedious voyage could do something like that!"

"Now you're just being modest," Tom said.

"No I'm not."

"Oh, then you're just trying to make me out to be an idiot then?" Tom said. "If I memorized pi up to about 30 digits, my brain would be lying in a puddle on the floor!" Joshua laughed. "And *forget* about me reciting them back a year later!"

"Okay, okay! What do you want me to do? Admit I'm *special?*" Joshua replied. "*You're* the one who's always teaching me every person has equal worth!"

"But not equal *gifts*," Tom said. "*Most* humans only use ten percent of their brains at any given moment. They tend to focus on the lobes they currently have need of using and not much else. When you were eleven, I observed you watching someone play the piano down in the rec room. It was an extremely difficult piece— Rachmaninov, I believe—and when the room cleared out, you went straight to the piano and played it, note-for-note. Do you realize now many of your brain lobes must have been simultaneously involved in that process? You were using your occipital lobe to watch his finger motion, your temporal lobe to listen to the sounds and store the information, your prefrontal area must have been *maxed-out* concentrating and storing motor skills you hadn't *personally* acquired, and your parietal lobe was probably in overdrive processing all this sensory input!"

"Was I breathing at the time?" Josh asked.

"Oh, did I leave out your brain stem? Gee whiz!"

Joshua laughed. "Dad, I know you're being polite and all, but to me, this is just the way… I am! It's never seemed out-of-the-ordinary, because I've never known any different. This is my *normal!*"

"Well, it's not normal to me. Or anyone else, for that matter. And the thing is… I haven't even told you the most impressive thing to me," Tom said.

"What's that?"

"You can glance into a crowd of people and know how each person feels by reading their nonverbal cues.

Then, *amazingly*, you know just how to appeal to those feelings! But it never feels like you're doing it to manipulate anyone; you just want to make their situation better. Your behavior toward them acknowledges your belief we're all equal and entitled to happiness. You are truly empathetic! Most savants on Earth were unable to properly connect with their *own* emotions, much less *others*! You *can*! I believe God has a plan for you."

"At least the Council does," Joshua acknowledged.

"They've got a plan for *all* of you. But God and I know *you* are destined to do great things."

Joshua sat and thought about that for a second. Just then, a knock came at the hatch and Tom bade whomever stood outside to enter. The door opened, and a giant man with a tag on his jumpsuit that read, "Brand: Lead Engineer," came in.

"Is this the same little Joshy that was filling his pants just a few years ago?" Brand asked. Joshua gave his father a look as if to say, *I soiled my pants just like everyone else, Dad.* Of course, it was ridiculous to expect his dad to read *that* in an expression.

"The same one," Tom replied.

"Holy smokes. What are you, twelve now?" Brand asked Joshua, tussling his hair with an enormous hand.

"Fourteen," Joshua said. He straightened up to look a little taller and fixed his hair.

"Wow! I can't believe it's been that long. You lose track of time in space!"

"What can we do for you, old friend?" Tom asked.

"Well, the Speaker wanted the maintenance crew to go around and remind everyone to meet in the chambers at 1100 hours, so they could get a headcount before he made his address. Oh, and you're invited to stand up on the observation balcony for the ceremony, Tom."

"Will do," Tom said.

"See you then, Tom," Brand said. Before he exited, Brand pulled his hands up into fists, flicked his nose with his thumbs and landed a punch on Joshua's arm. It hurt, but Joshua pretended he didn't feel anything. The door closed behind Brand.

"You were probably calculating complex equations every time you pooped your diaper," Tom said to Joshua.

"Wow! You must be telepathic," Joshua said. His father didn't answer. "Dad?"

"Oh, you didn't hear my answer?" Tom said.

"I guess not, then." They laughed.

3

Darrell made his way to his best friend Josh's chamber. This might be the last day they had to hang out with each other. *Who knew if cryogenics even worked?* Darrell thought. *We might never wake up, and if that was the case…*

Darrell didn't want to think about that. They were supposed to live forever, or at least considerably longer than the human race ever had. No need to dwell on hypotheticals. There was still a little time for fun.

He and his peers had spent their entire lives on this ship. They were genetic creations, incubated into existence, and their "parents" were whichever scientists were available to train them in the disciplines the Council deemed necessary for the new world. Many of them were raised in nurseries, and after they were old enough to begin training at ages 4 or 5, their "parents" took over. In some cases (like Darrell's), the relationship was more like an apprenticeship than a family. He spent his nights in the public sleeping quarters, with a few hundred others his age, and then arose and trained in the botanical wing for the duration of waking hours.

Nigel, his "father" was the lead botanist. He was

faithful in training Darrell in understanding how plant life interacts with other life forms. Darrell could build a small ecosystem in the UV garden capable of maintaining edibles symbiotic with Earth humans. They tried many different combinations to accommodate a variety of climes, sometimes pulling seeds from the cryogenic seed bank, other times working with Joshua to rotate in genetically-modified plants and monitor their behavior.

That's how he and Joshua became best friends. He preferred working with Joshua over the others, because working with Joshua just made Darrell feel smarter. Joshua could predict which combinations of plants would work together in perfect balance, but he would pose calculated questions to Darrell so it seemed like *he* came up with the answer on his own. He knew Josh was letting him take the credit, but it still made him feel good. *Anyone* who worked with Josh made decades of progress in weeks, but he was so good at making himself seem like just a cog in the gear-work, that his contributions went largely unrecognized. Being around him made a person feel better, act better, *be* better.

Darrell tapped on the hatch leading to Josh and Tom's quarters. The door slid open and there stood Tom, smiling. Darrell immediately felt a twinge of envy that Josh had such a great parent figure in his life.

"Hey, Mr. Hawker, is Josh around?" Darrell asked. Josh came up behind Tom. Tom stayed in front of Josh, almost sentry-like.

"What's up, Darrell?" Josh said.

"Notta lotta. Want to go for one last jaunt?" Josh looked at his dad for permission. Tom looked reluctant to let him go, but he stepped aside after a pause.

"Don't get into trouble," Tom said. "And be back in time for the ceremony."

"Will do, Dad," Josh said. With that, he fell in step with Darrell and they hurried down the corridor. Josh seemed to know right where Darrell was going to take him when they made a few turns.

They stopped in front of a keypad-entry door that read, "Authorized Personnel Only: No Admittance." For years, whenever Josh and Darrell would prematurely finish a project that should have taken months, they would pretend to be going to the computer lab to enter their findings into the publication database. Instead, they explored the massive ship. They worked their way through all of the maintenance corridors, following the dim, labyrinthine passages that brought electricity, air and liquids to various parts of the ship. Josh could hold all the different elements in his head like a map, and when they got back to the lab, he would draw out the schematics on paper.

They would spy on other labs through the observation windows and vents, pretending like they were uncovering great conspiracies and saving the day. They would invent stories, setting themselves up to be heroes in every scenario. Sometimes they would be caught sneaking around by maintenance personnel and escorted out into the main corridors, but after a while they got to be pretty good at hiding when someone came around. It seemed they knew the passageways better than the technicians. Part of this was due to the hand-drawn map Joshua kept in his pocket. He pulled it out now. Darrell couldn't make heads or tails of it: It looked to him like random colors and shapes. But Josh *could* read it, and he claimed he drew it this way to protect them if someone discovered it. Very spy-like, even if it *was* probably made up.

"Today, we become 'authorized personnel', by virtue of putting our lives at risk for the continuation of the human race," Darrell announced. "We're going to explore The Elite's quarters and uncover why our food sucks so bad."

"And how do you propose we get in?" Josh asked.

"Well, that's what I brought you along for," Darrell said. "Come on, genius, do your thing!"

Josh touched the screen of the entry pad and a

grid of nine dots came up. Darrell knew the sort of code this was; there was a similar code outside of his lab. You had to connect a number of dots in some way to unlock the door. But he had no idea how Josh would break this code. It wasn't like a number code, where if you knew something about the person who encoded it, you could guess at which number sequences would be meaningful to them, like birthdays, anniversaries and such. This door also set off an alarm if the code was entered incorrectly even once, that's how important it was for The Elites to stay separated. Josh stared for a second, then moved to the side and stared at the glassy surface of the keypad.

"What you thinking, boss?" Darrell asked.

"People's fingers are naturally oily, so I'm trying to see if there are streaks I can see on the surface of the screen. I'm trying to line my angle up so the light from the ceiling reflects off the surface and… there it is. Come stand right here." Darrell squatted down and could see a shape like an hourglass without the top line.

"Well, that answers what shape to make. Now the question is, where to start?" Darrell said.

Josh thought for a moment. "Animals can't talk, right?" Josh asked.

"They can communicate," Darrell answered.

"Yeah, but I mean talk intelligently, using language

and logic like humans can."

"Uh-huh. Where are you going with this?"

"Which hemisphere of the brain controls our language?" Josh asked.

"The left hemisphere."

"And that controls which side of the body?"

"The right side."

"Yes," said Josh. "Did you know animals don't have a preference for handedness?"

"I guess I do now."

"Because humans have the ability to use language, about 70 to 90 percent of us are…"

"Right-handed," Darrell finished. "So chances are pretty good that whoever encoded this door was right-handed."

"You see where I'm going with this, now?"

"Yeah," Darrell said. "You think the handedness of a person will determine where on the keypad they start. But don't we all write left-to-right anyway?"

"Yes, we do," said Josh. "But this isn't writing: This is a drawing. Left-handed people would subconsciously train themselves to draw right-to-left, to avoid smudging their hand across their drawings. So considering all this, the drawing starts on the…"

"Left, like I said," Darrell said. He started swiping

the code into the keypad.

"Right."

"Right?" Darrell stopped in mid-swipe worried he might have messed it up.

"No, I mean correct. Affirmative," Josh laughed at him. Darrell gathered himself and finished the code. The light above the door turned green and it opened.

"Man, you had me sweating bullets," Darrell said. Josh just kept laughing, but quieted down once they stepped inside. They looked around the larger corridor and saw there was nobody there. The corridor had actual carpet on the floors and sconces on the wall casting a comforting, warm light.

"Talk about upper crust," Darrell whispered. Josh was too busy looking around to respond to his comment.

"There," Josh whispered, and they both scampered over to a panel on the far wall. The maintenance hatches in this section of the ship were not clearly labeled, but Josh had noticed a small handle on one of the wainscoting panels, and was now attempting to open it. It slid upward out of its retention slot and then swung in on hinges. Darrell and Josh had to crawl in, and then they shut the hatch behind them.

Inside, Darrell pulled out his flashlight and they

looked around. The curve of the passageway mimicked the curve of the corridor outside, with the exception that it was dark and they had to hunch over to keep from hitting their heads.

"Which way do you think takes us to the Council's chambers?" Darrell whispered. Josh looked at the conduits surrounding them, and glancing at his map, deduced the direction they should go was to their right. They made their way toward the Council's chambers, sometimes having to climb up or down ladders. Darrell could see Josh memorizing the layout of everything.

They soon came to a spot where they could hear voices. They had to lie down in order to see through the grate into the Council's chambers. A gathering of about twenty people sat around a large table, discussing something. Darrell strained to hear what was being said. "...set for blackout, except for life support and engines once we're in," said a man with a beard.

"What if Alpha fails?" a woman said.

"It won't make a difference then, will it?" replied the man. "I guess the only difference would then be to turn off life support everywhere."

"And just willingly welcome death?" she objected.

"This is a survival mission," another person interjected. "I agree with DeAnne. We don't need to quit because it failed once. We start again, with new subjects. We'll still have the greatest minds from Earth in our circle, as well as all the information in the publication database."

Someone in a lab coat stood up. "Our resources are highly limited. We would not have very long before we were forced to make harder decisions."

"Like which of *us* gets to wait for you to figure it out?" DeAnne asked. A murmur of conversation erupted. A man dressed in a robe with a bright stole stood up and pounded a gavel on the table. Darrell recognized him as the Council Speaker.

"Quiet down!" he demanded. They stopped speaking. "We're speaking in hypotheticals! What's the use of worrying about something we have no answer to? Early indications are that Alpha will work! We can bump up the timeline for a wellness check if time is everyone's main concern."

"I don't like waiting," a man said. "It's not like we're getting any younger. I second that idea."

"Very well, then," the Speaker said. "All in favor of moving up the timeline?" Everyone raised their hands. "Any objections?" Nobody objected. "Then it's settled. I will change the settings at the commencement. Any other items of business?" Nobody spoke.

"Okay, then...meeting adjourned. Please make sure you're in place on time, and be in good spirits, for the sake of the children." They got up to leave.

"Sounds bigger than food," Darrell whispered.

"Yeah."

"What do you think this meeting was about?"

"I'm not entirely sure," Josh said.

They explored for a few more hours, then decided to start heading back. As they neared the panel they first crawled into, Darrell pulled out his time capsule.

"Josh, I put some stuff in a vacuum-sealed capsule. I think I want to hide it in here and see if it survives through hibernation."

"You know you're only going to be a day older, right?" Josh asked.

"Yeah, but I'll be *so* much wiser," Darrell joked. Then he added solemnly, "But in case I'm not around to open it...you know."

"I understand," Josh said. They looked around for a secret place to stash his capsule, and found a spot where it wedged snugly behind a panel box.

"It's about time we checked back in," Darrell said.

"Yep. Bedtime," Josh said.

4

The Darwin Generation milled about on the main floor of the spacious cryogenic wing, being surrounded by the Council and the other crewmembers in the upper observation decks.

Lining the curved walls, the bedchambers were opened like hundreds of hungry coffins. Joshua looked up and located his father standing above him to the right. He gave his dad a thumbs up and a smile, hoping that would give his father the illusion that he was calm. His father's gaze never wandered from Joshua. He was not speaking with the other adults, just watching. He gave a melancholy smile and thumbs up in return. Someone from behind punched Josh in his arm.

"I wonder if you'll wake up with a bruise in four-hundred-some-odd years?" Darrell was standing behind him rubbing his knuckles.

"I was wondering the same thing about a black eye," replied Joshua. He feinted a punch and Darrell flinched.

"Whoa, take it easy, slugger! I'm trained in hand-to-nad combat, remember?"

"As long as you're still claiming to be male, I guess I am, too," Joshua replied. Darrell laughed, but it was an uneasy laugh. Josh could see he was nervous, too. "So…your training in botany ought to come in handy when we wake up and need to study the plant life of our new home. Think about it, you'll be employed on day one!"

"Don't worry. I'll give you a job as a taste-tester! Somebody's got to find out which plants won't kill us, right?"

A pretty brunette named Tara overheard their conversation and chimed in. "If feeding people plants and waiting to see if they die is the extent of your training, Darrell, an Earth caveman could do it."

This was the first time Tara had spoken so casually to Joshua. Technically, she was speaking to Darrell, but it still made Joshua feel special that he was Darrell's friend.

"Not all of us can be chemists," said Joshua. She looked at him funny.

"*You* could."

"Yeah, Josh," said Darrell. "You're not fooling anyone with this 'pretending to be normal' thing. We all know you're a genius. How many times has the Speaker *personally* given you a scientific merit award? Let's see… carry the one…"

Joshua could feel his face getting flush.

Fortunately, the awkward moment was interrupted by the Council Speaker.

"Welcome, everyone!" The chamber went quiet. "As we're all aware, today is Sleep Day; the day we put all of humanity's hopes into cryogenic sleep, only to awaken in four hundred seventy- two years to a new home!" The Speaker waited for the applause to die before continuing.

"We have trained each of you in specialties designed to give us the greatest shot at making planet Hope habitable. We have given you genetic traits we do not possess ourselves to prolong your lives and make you less susceptible to disease. We have raised you as if you were our own children. We have bled, sweat, and cried over you. Now all that is left is for us to hope the proximity alarms wake you up when the planet is near!" There was some nervous laughter.

"As you know, we will not be alive when you awaken at the end of the journey. So this is goodbye. A few technicians will awaken you after 20 years to check your vitals and then put you back into stasis, but beyond that, you are on your own now. Stay true to your training in the scientific disciplines, and you will be successful. We have made you not only fit to survive, but to thrive. Continue to evolve, Darwin Generation!"

The Speaker returned to his place among the

Council after gesturing for them to start getting into their bedchambers. A lone voice called out from the decks, and Joshua recognized it as his father's.

"God be with you."

The Speaker looked over at Tom and said, "If '*God*' was with *anyone*, we'd still be on Earth."

Joshua could see his father's gaze still fixed on him as he climbed into the bed and the technician connected hoses to his cryo-suit. They injected the anesthetic into his neck and closed the glass lid. When all the kids were secured, Joshua watched as the Speaker stood up and punched a code into the console. Then he read the Speaker's lips as he announced, "Project Alpha is underway!"

Joshua made one more important connection. He put his fists together in the shape of a brain and desperately hoped his father was still watching him. Then he slept.

5

"Wake up!"

Joshua opened his eyes. It felt as if he had *just* went to sleep moments before. The sensation of losing time that way was unsettling. His father stood over him, dressed in a cryo-tech's suit. Joshua was relieved to see his dad wasn't twenty years older. Maybe only a few years older?

"Dad! The Speaker is not a cryogenicist! He's a politician from Earth: What business does he have entering dates into the system?"

"Shhhh," Tom warned as he unhooked his son's suit. Through the fog in the room, Joshua could see others nearby being disconnected by technicians. He realized his father was here in disguise and this was a rescue operation. At Joshua's prompting, his dad must have looked deeper into the Council's plans, and drawn the same conclusion Joshua had as he was being put into stasis. He realized he needed to go along with his father's act.

They fell into line with the others being led down the corridor to the medical labs. Partway down, his father looked behind him, and seeing nobody coming, broke off and took Joshua to a maintenance door. Tom tapped on the door. Another cryo-tech came around the corner, leading a group of his peers that included Darrell.

"Hey, Josh, I guess we'll be *two* days older! Are you coming?" Darrell asked. Tom kept his head down and pretended to be adjusting something on Joshua's cryo-suit.

"Yeah, I'll be there," Josh responded. Then he quickly added, "Thanks for being my best friend. I love you, Darrell."

"O-o-kay?" Darrell said. "The drugs still affecting you?" Then he disappeared with the group around the bend.

The door opened, and there stood Brand, who ushered them in quickly and closed the door behind them. They started walking down the maintenance passageway, which Joshua recognized as one leading to the rear of the ship. Only then did Tom speak openly. "Joshua, you were right to be concerned! They had no intention of keeping you in the chambers until we reached the planet. Genetic modifications to prolong life were *always* Plan B! If we couldn't figure out cryogenic sleep on the voyage, *then* genetic modifications would come into play with another generation, but only as a last resort."

"It looks like Plan Alpha works," said Joshua, solemnly. "How long did they wait before they decided to check our vitals?"

"It's only been a year. And your friends don't know it. They think this is the twenty-year checkup. As soon as the Council gets the results, the Darwin Generation loses its ticket to ride, and the Council takes *their* scientists into stasis along with them."

"We were fools to think we had any value beyond being glorified guinea pigs," Joshua said. "How could we expect anything different from a group of powerful people from Earth who would force a man to leave his family because his family had no worth to *them*. It's all about survival of the fittest."

"More like 'might makes right,'" Tom said. The technician led them down the darkened maintenance corridor until they came to a narrow plexiglass window. "Do you know where we are?" he asked Joshua.

He looked out and recognized the air lock for disposing waste. "Yes," he said. It was a large room with a mechanical hatch which would open to empty space. Hundreds of his peers stood in the room, stripped of their cryo-suits and looking frightened. A few more, including Darrell, were led in at gunpoint, not by technicians but Special Forces agents. The vitals tests must have been successful.

"Cowards!" Brand said. "They can't imagine

trusting these kids with their lives, because they don't trust *themselves* with these kids' lives. They can't fathom anyone acting any differently, so they have to eliminate them!" They watched as a few more were ushered in.

"Elise… your mom, liked to garden," Tom said. The words seemed disconnected to what was happening. Joshua looked over at his dad, who had tears welling up in his eyes. "She would spend hours every day in the summer, pulling weeds, spraying, watering. She tried to get me to do it with her, but I was always too busy. But in the fall, she would bring in the most beautiful produce and would make salads for your brothers and sister and me. Fried zucchini, corn on the cob, baked potatoes, she shared it all with us.

"Oh, and the strawberries! They were so sweet! I wish you could taste a strawberry! Your mom had a whole section of the garden dedicated to her strawberry patch." He paused for a moment, reflecting.

"We had this word. Myoki-achiaba. You won't find it in any dictionary because it doesn't exist in any language. It only meant anything to the two of us. We made it up one day when we were just… happy. It started out as just something silly and nonsensical, just… us having fun, but then it evolved into something deeper. It came to mean, I love you, and you love me. Something *only* the two of us shared and understood. But we did it together, and that's all that mattered. You're the first person I've ever said this to, besides her.

"I prayed that God would deliver my family. Deliver them to a place with rich, soft soil. A place she could call her own. I never… I never got to tell her goodbye." He wept openly now.

Joshua came over and threw his arms around his dad. He realized his dad was trying to connect him to his Earth family, and give him the gift of a real mother.

"Thanks for telling me about mom," he said. "Myoki-achiaba."

"Myoki-achiaba," His dad repeated.
The technicians closed and sealed the door behind the last of the Darwin Generation. Brand looked at Tom, who wiped his tears and started toward the maintenance door connected to the main ship.

"Dad," said Joshua. "What are you going to do?"

"Whatever I can," Tom said. "Brand, make sure he stays out of sight."

"Will do," Brand said.

"Those are SF agents down there!" Joshua protested. "They are the highest level of security on this ship! You won't last a minute against them!"

"I have to try *something*." Tom said, solemnly. He didn't look away from the door. "Goodbye, my son. Be good."

Tom went through the door and Joshua heard it click behind him. He came into view again, charging the agent getting ready to open the airlock behind his friends, who were now pounding on the door and pleading to be let back in. The man heard Tom's approach and wheeled just before Tom reached him. His dad had no combat training, so it was only a matter of seconds before his dad's frail body was cast to the ground by the muscular guard. Joshua tried to run toward the door, but Brand caught him with his large hands and held him fast. There was a flash of light, and Joshua watched in shock as his dad's body went suddenly limp. Another agent came over and stood guard as his father's killer arose and pulled the airlock release. In a silent, dreamlike moment, everyone Joshua had grown up with was gone, jettisoned into space like trash.

When the airlock was closed and refilled with air, the technicians moved his father's lifeless body into the room, and he lay there solitary, until the hatch was reopened.

Joshua sobbed into Brand's chest.

6

Joshua's hand hovered over the life-support controls to the Speaker's cryogenic chamber.

It would be so easy.

Joshua was literally an inch away from avenging the deaths of his father and closest friends. They had not signed onto this mission as guinea pigs. They didn't deserve to die in the horrible manner they did, much less for the reason of preserving an elite, self-centered class of humanity.

Just push abort.

Joshua was convinced that many of the worst traits of humanity had made it onto the ship to escape Earth. The people whose value was measured in power, money, influence, or deception.

After millennia of humans trying to overcome "survival of the fittest" behaviors in order to create a peaceful civilization with law and order, *this* was what would survive.

He won't even feel pain. It'll be just like dying in his sleep.

He lifted his stinging eyes from the console to look at the other chambers, all filled with council members, their families, and their support personnel. Not an empty chamber. Only enough to house everyone *they* deemed worthy of salvation. But only because they were valuable to The Elites. Joshua now knew why there were only so many of the Darwin Generation created. There were only so many beds to carry out the testing...

All of them deserve to die if they can't see the value of anyone beyond their own noses!

One hot tear streamed down his cheek. He thought he had cried all he could. These tears were different; angry, bitter tears, heavy with salt. He tried to understand why his hand didn't follow his emotions. Why did the inch between his finger and the console feel like a mile? Was it because he had never killed anyone before? Was the idea of ending someone's life who had spent an entire lifetime preserving it somehow unthinkable? It's not as if the Speaker had shown any restraint when it came to putting his plan in motion to kill others. The moment the Speaker casually punched in the cryo-chamber initialization code sprang to Joshua's mind.

There was no remorse on his face.

Perhaps logic stayed his hand. That nagging "reason" that halted his emotions. He took a moment to examine his logic, since it seemed so desperate to prevent him from acting out the urge that filled his entire body and spilled out in gasps and sobs. This was a survival mission; the only one that Joshua knew of. If he were to eliminate The Elites in their sleep, the chances of humanity's survival decreased considerably. Instead of just committing homicides, he might ultimately be committing xenocide.

Just one person, then. The one most deserving of death.
Him.

Joshua only needed one bed, anyway. He was not accounted for when the remainder went into stasis, and it was only because of Brand that Joshua knew how to keep some of the ship's life- support systems on when the power was diverted to only the bedchambers and engines. Now he looked at all those asleep while he stayed awake, alone. His own will to survive still made him consider desperate actions unfamiliar to him. The motivation for revenge made this leap smaller.

Logic vs. emotion, and emotion carried all the weight of his soul.

Survival of the fittest, right? Their code, not mine. Live by the sword...

Joshua pressed his finger down on the console.

7

Down a maintenance corridor in The Elite's quarters, Joshua pulled a capsule out from behind a panel box. He remembered Darrell's fear of dying in cryogenic sleep, and his misplaced faith in those who would ultimately kill him. A combination of Darrell's fears and hopes were probably what prompted him to make this capsule.

Joshua climbed out of the access hatch and absently walked to the observation deck, watching the capsule clutched in his hands, as if he was afraid to lose it. The observation deck was located at the "top" of the ship, according to the simulated gravity. It protruded from the ship as did the flight deck, to give a 360-degree view of space, as well as a view of the stars directly above him. He never had access to this room before Brand gave him the master code and went to sleep. Now this, as well as any other space on the ship, was his alone.

Joshua quickly punched in commands on the master control panel that sealed the door behind him and diverted continuing life-support to this room. He landed heavily in a swiveling armchair.

The capsule Darrell had used was a vacuum-sealed capsule from the seed nursery. He broke the seal with a loud pop, pulled up the chair's desk and dumped the contents onto it. Some of the items gyrated strangely as they expanded in their new-found freedom. The first thing he noticed was a photograph printed out on plastic. A younger, smiling Darrell stood with his arm around the shoulders of a younger him. Joshua instantly recalled the day this was shot; when the head botanist celebrated the two of them creating their first self-sustaining ecosystem, *way* ahead of schedule. Joshua put this photo into his breast pocket.

Also in the capsule were two vials—one of small seeds, one of blood (probably Darrell's)—which he also pocketed. Some other things held no meaning for Joshua; a copper pin with what looked like a rune engraved on it— similar in shape to a number four, but with a line crossing the bottom stem—a small rubber ball, a hairpin, a toy model of a fighter ship, a scenic picture of a forest on Earth, ripped from one of his texts. Darrell had always dreamed of living in a world with plant-life, and he had a particular affinity for evergreen trees. He had told Joshua he admired their variety and their ability to thrive in colder climates. They had always looked strong to Darrell, stretching up into the open skies of Earth.

The last thing in the capsule was a piece of paper, folded a number of times into a tiny square-like pocket. On one side of it was written, "For Joshua," in his father's handwriting. His father must have known about the capsule and given this to Darrell. Joshua unfolded it, expecting a letter of some sort. Instead, it was just a blank, gray sheet of paper. He flipped it over; nothing. Was this one last prank from Darrell?

Joshua looked closer at the paper and noticed tiny rows, microscopic lines giving the paper its gray color. He turned on the desk, changed the camera settings to "macro," and flipped the paper over onto the tiny camera. He could see a series of ones and zeroes. Binary code. He switched the camera mode to "scan" and started scanning lines of code into the computer. After about an hour of doing this, he reached the end. The saved files he converted to text and then attempted to open the file with every application. It didn't seem long enough to be a video file, but could have been a short clip if the file was low quality and compressed. No luck with any movie codecs. Next he tried audio codecs, and when that proved unsuccessful, he tried image codecs, then text codecs. Then he tried everything else. Databasing software, flight control applications, navigation software, life-support systems applications, even *games*. Nothing.

Joshua couldn't wrap his head around why his dad would give him worthless code.

Without an existing program to decode with, this paper was nothing but a series of "on/not on" commands. His father's code was so well written, it would remain a secret from *everyone*, especially now that the coder was dead. Any code without a receiver defeated the purpose. Joshua wadded up the paper and threw it into the trash receptacle, frustrated.

He was tired. He wished he could sleep dreamlessly through the voyage the way the Speaker and the Council were. His decision to press "cancel" and leave the Speaker alive lifted the heavy burden of anger from his shoulders, but left him with a survival dilemma of his own. There were no bedchambers for him to sleep in, and he didn't know how long—if *any* longer—his genetic modifications would prolong his life. The Elites didn't exactly let this experiment play out.

What exactly did the bedchambers *do*, anyway? Joshua remembered listening to some technicians through a vent on one of his and Darrell's outings, and heard them briefly discussing the dilemma of slowing the human functions through freezing enough to slow all processes down without stopping them completely. One meant prolonging life and the other meant instant death. It was a fine line to walk for such a drastic difference in outcomes.

He stared out at the stars. They didn't move, even though they were traveling at the speed of light. Straight to the aft of the ship was Sol, the yellow dwarf star humanity left behind. Directly to the stern of the ship was Keppler-186, the star around which planet Hope orbited. These were the only fixed points in their voyage, but it still seemed like they were frozen in space and time. Distance from the ship prevented the stars from moving across his field of vision. Joshua fixed his gaze on one star to the left of the ship. He was *done* thinking, *done* moving, *done* trying! He just wanted to stare at the star. Staring, staring, staring.

Without him realizing it at first, the star started to slowly make a path across the observation pane, as well as those around it. He saw the change in position, but the instant he tried to qualify the experience with a worded question in his head, the stars once again became immobile.

Joshua felt stiff. He looked down at his body and a sprinkling of dandruff fell from his head. His arms were coated with a thin layer of dust as well. He brushed off his arms and wondered what he had just experienced. He achingly got to his feet and felt the need to stretch. The stretching felt invigorating, but he soon was aware of a stabbing hunger for food and water, as well as a desperate need to urinate.

Joshua relieved himself in a nearby lavatory, ate a food packet, drained a canteen of water, and tried to comprehend why the stars seemed to move suddenly. *Of course*, the stars were fixed in space and the *ship* was moving, but why did it move *faster*? Then Joshua made a connection: The ship *didn't* move faster, *he* did!

Joshua knew time perception was a function of the left hemisphere of the brain. He remembered times when he was younger, caught up in a drawing, when time seemed to fly by. Since he was so focused on a right-hemisphere function, strictly dealing with spatial awareness and ignoring language, the function of timekeeping in his left hemisphere turned off. It was the same reason six hours of sleep could seem like minutes on a dreamless night. In that case, *both* of his brain hemispheres temporarily ceased to function as they did when he was conscious.

But had he really just passed through time at a different rate?

He wanted to test his theory. In case this worked, Joshua decided he should reseal Darrell's keepsakes in the vacuum capsule and deposit them in their original hiding place behind the panel in the Elites' maintenance corridor away from oxygen in order to preserve them. Then he jogged down to the medical wing and grabbed some monitors, an IV drip, a catheter, and a timer, and then he returned to the observation deck and connected the monitors to him. He was inexperienced with finding a vein with a needle, but he had seen it done on him enough times that he got the needle fixed in place after only three painful tries. Inserting the catheter made the IV needle feel like a Swedish massage in comparison.

After that, he connected the heart monitor, neurosensors, and blood-pressure cuff, then set the timer to zero and pushed start. Then, settling the chair back in a reclining position, he tried to go into a meditative state.

Focus, on the star, Josh. Focus… focus… focus.

He repeated the mantra in his mind while he watched the star. Joshua sat for about an hour, according to the timer, before he sat up in frustration.

Why aren't the stars moving? Joshua asked himself. *What am I doing wrong?*

Speaking.

It was ironic that it was the very hemisphere responsible for his failure that provided him with the answer to his question. He realized the left hemisphere also controlled language. As long as he engaged his left hemisphere with words, he couldn't slip into his comatose-like state. He reset the timer, reclined himself, and tried again.

Joshua had to consciously make an effort to drown out the thoughts in his head. Every time he told himself to remove the words from his thought processes, he realized he was using words to instruct himself. He had to completely empty himself, as he had felt emptied before. He fixed his eyes on a star and *just* existed.

Staring, staring, staring... This time, the stars moved.

8

One month at a time was about all Joshua's body could handle. He was awake for about one hour in between "naps," and during that time, he would relieve himself, eat, and exercise in order for his muscles not to atrophy. In each room he visited, he increased the pull of the artificial gravity to train his legs for a larger planet.

The monitors told him he had essentially accomplished naturally what the cryogenic chambers had to do artificially. He had slowed his heartbeat down to about one beat per minute, as well as put into stasis all of his other bodily functions, including aging. In two years' time, he had only aged one day. At the end of the voyage, he would only be about 8 months older at that rate.

It seemed a strange way to live; exercising and performing basic bodily functions, separated by about 15 minutes of meditation. Rinse, repeat.

He found he didn't need sleep in the traditional sense. The time spent meditating took care of everything sleep normally accomplished, but it was a strange feeling never losing total consciousness. He needed to watch the stars move in order for him to know he was perceiving time at a different rate. Perhaps this was unnecessary, but it was the only method he knew, so he stuck with it. Although he *was* becoming aware of changes in his body, without having to name them. He just *felt* different when he passed time.

Sometimes during his awake hours, he would visit other parts of the ship and check on things.

He would even stop in on the cryogenic chamber and check on the vitals of those in cryogenic sleep, even though he knew there were technicians whom the computer would awaken at intervals to do just that. He began to feel a stewardship over the ship and its passengers. Their survival was the survival of humanity. As he looked at the peaceful, resting faces of those in sleep, he could imagine their mothers watching them sleep when they were newborns, loving them without condition.

At first, he pitied them, clinging so desperately to life they would do anything to preserve their own. They were scared of death. Even though he had no convictions of an afterlife, his father's death taught him not to fear death so much. Either he would see his father again in another form, or he would cease to exist and, therefore, not be around to care that he wasn't around. Despite his nonchalant attitude about death, he didn't seek it. Life was still interesting to him, and he wasn't sure he was done with it.

After a while, Joshua grew tired of the generic exercise routine he did to keep his body strong. He decided to start doing exercise he could *use,* if need be. He accessed the ship's massive database of information siphoned from Earth's internet servers and started watching tutorials on self-defense and hand-to-hand combat techniques. Earth had combined many techniques into one effective discipline called "mixed martial arts," but upon watching many bouts in this discipline, he was unimpressed with how balanced many matches were. He needed to have an immediate, effective advantage over any potential opponent, so he decided he would start over and research the roots of this discipline in order to create his own style.

Sometimes he would stay up longer than his normal hour studying various techniques and training himself in the gym using dummies. In his studies, he was impressed with the grace and beauty of Wu-Shu, but quickly realized the choreographed nature of it that had evolved over centuries served little purpose outside of tradition. There was a martial artist named Bruce Lee who took traditional kung-fu and eliminated the patterned motions in favor of quick, forward strikes, creating a style he called "Jeet Kune Do." Fortunately, there were many videos of Bruce Lee available since he was also a cinema actor. He could sift through the choreographed nature of the fight scenes and just focus on Lee's technique.

He also studied wrestling techniques from every nation and culture, starting with ancient Greece and moving through the last Olympics. He was impressed with a country named Iran's dominance in the sport, both at Greco-Roman wrestling and Freestyle. The first style required the athletes to take down an opponent utilizing locks and leverage in the upper body, and the second style normally focused on controlling the legs of an opponent in order to gain an advantage.

He studied the throws of Judo, the power striking of Karate, Muay Thai's use of elbows and knees, the balance and leverage of Sumo, the defense of boxing, the submissions of Brazilian Jiu-Jitsu, and the strongest parts of lesser-known techniques and combined all of these into one style befitting his size and body-type. He was able to stimulate the motor-skills lobe in his brain when he practiced each technique, making muscle memory in a few repetitions where others had taken a lifetime in perfecting these techniques.

Thus Joshua created a fighting style uniquely his own.

Joshua spent the rest of his waking time learning all he could about every subject he thought would benefit him, and planning for the time when the rest of the ship would awaken. He discovered he had the ability to process words visually by shutting off the auditory function of his brain, so he could blow through volumes of research in minutes. He perused the science databases and gleaned as much as he could from theories that had not yet been disproven. Many studies were published without the researcher becoming familiar with previous studies that had already disproven his or her theory. Joshua didn't know if this was because of ineptitude, laziness or agenda, but he started mapping out in his head all the likely "true" theories and how they connected to truth in other scientific fields. He had to know how humans affected their environments, how the environment affected them, and how they interacted socially (in which the study of history and psychology proved invaluable). Pseudoscience and incorrect theories were easy to identify and discard because of their inability to fit in with the big picture. He was aware that very few individuals ever connected economics with microbiology, sociology with botany, philosophy with zoology, or archaeology with physics, because of the specialized nature of Earth's universities. He had the advantage of freedom to direct his own studies, and he could see the connecting force between all these fields.

Man.

It was through Man's lens that all of these things were observed. Without the ability to reason, there could be no sciences. Animals simply exist within the sphere in which they were created. They spend no time trying to understand the universe around them, they just... are, Joshua thought.

The observation made him feel special. Not because of anything he accomplished individually, but because he was endowed with the ability to reason.

How did Man get this power? Evolution clearly happened on Earth, but what could possibly cause the vast evolutionary leap between monkey and man?

It was a difference measured with every thought in his head. He realized there had *never* been a chimpanzee on Earth contemplating the philosophical reasons for the differences between it and Man. And Joshua was unaware of any intelligence filling the gap between the two. Then another thought occurred to him, and a gap was filled. He made a connection from all his readings on primate biomechanics, fossil records, mythology, and ecology niches which would have angered the academic types back on Earth, but simply made him laugh: *Bigfoot was real!*

9

His dad stood over him, smiling.

It was just a brief moment, but as soon as Joshua noticed him, he immediately formed the worded question in his mind that brought him out of stasis, and the image of his father disappeared.

Did I really just see Dad, or did my brain dream this up?

Despite his strong desire to answer the question, he didn't experience anything like that for the next few sleeps, and therefore concluded the latter.

———————————

Joshua started to notice differences in the observation room. Because he needed continual oxygen in the room, some of the less-permanent objects were biodegrading. The leather on the chairs was dry and cracked, and the pneumatics in the chairs no longer functioned because of the decaying rubber gaskets. He did a quick calculation in his head and realized he had covered about 238 years of the voyage.

Joshua began sleeping in other areas, each time sealing the doors and diverting life support to that room.

Since the Elites weren't currently using their quarters, it made for an ideal place for him to spend a few dozen years in flight. When any signs of aging began to take place, he would leave the room and vacuum the oxygen out to be recycled, and then find another room.

After a while, he ventured from the rooms and decided to find a more permanent place to stay which wouldn't decay as much. It occurred to him that he had never explored the ventilation system fully, since the giant room in which the oxygen was produced was strictly off-limits to humans. They didn't want people in this room, in case someone should contaminate their limited, pure air source. Joshua was curious as to how they produced the oxygen in the first place.

He found he didn't need his map to navigate the ship—it was all in his head, just as it had been on paper—which was a good thing since the paper had yellowed, crackled and disintegrated about 150 voyage years ago.

He walked to the central hub of the oxygen chamber, but could see no entrance into it. He would have to access it through the ventilation ducts. He found a grate nearby and opened it, scooting into the duct on his belly. It led to a large, cylindrical chamber, which had large fans in the bottom, moving the air to other parts of the ship. The vents leading to other sections of the ship which were not

currently supporting life were shut tightly. Only the rooms
he was currently diverting life support to had open ducts.
The only other openings were near the top of the chamber,
where the oxygen was produced. Pulling up the map in his
mind, he wondered why this space was so large, compared
to other mechanical systems.

He climbed the ladder and entered through one of
the openings. Inside, he discovered the answer to his
question. He stood upright and marveled at the forest of
trees now before him. The giant room was dark, lit only by
starlight streaming in from a clear ceiling above. He
estimated in his head that the space was probably seven
square acres. He felt his way along the walls, trying to
minimize contamination to any of the plant-life that
produced oxygen for the people of the ship. The floor felt
strange, and when he bent down, he saw it was made of
grass. He couldn't help brushing through it with his hand.
It was unlike anything he had ever felt before!

He wondered how these plants were fed with
sunlight and water this far out in space. These resources
were in limited quantities. He closed his eyes and thought
through all the systems he had encountered in his
explorations of the ship. He recalled seeing hydrogen
collectors on the outside of the ship, collecting the tiny
atoms of hydrogen that were present in "empty" space, and

storing them in pressurized containers. These containers were connected to this chamber, which created oxygen. The combination of these elements created enough water to feed the life aboard this ship. The remaining oxygen was used for breathing, and the trees were fed with the carbon dioxide the humans breathed out.

But that still didn't account for sunlight. As if in answer to his question, blinding lights came on in the room. Starlight captured with the most sensitive of solar panels on the outside of the ship must have been stored up as energy to be released in bright bursts to feed these trees. The lights had to equal the color temperature and lumens of the Earth's sun, as well as transfer UV rays, so this was the brightest light Joshua had ever beheld. He shaded and squinted his eyes for a few minutes until his vision adjusted to the sudden change from night to day.

He could now see well enough to walk along the circular wall without having to feel his way. Every once in a while, branches would impede his way and he would have to walk out onto the grass. He removed his shoes to try to keep the grass clean, and he found he really enjoyed the sensation of walking barefoot on grass. The cool, soft blades played between his toes and hugged his feet. He almost didn't want to get off.

Suddenly, he came to a door in the wall. It was

near where the elite's quarters would be. Specifically, it was nearest the Speaker's chamber, if not connected outright. A flush of anger filled him. He didn't care about contamination; all he cared about was privacy and exclusiveness! Besides being a vital function of the ship, this was a private garden for the privileged.

If that's the way he wants to play…

Joshua tossed his shoes aside and started running through the trees. He rubbed the rough bark of some trees and attempted to climb up others. It was all so… wild! Was this what Earth was like?

No, Earth would probably have far more diversity.

When he tired of running and climbing, Joshua decided to lie next to a large tree and pass some time in here. He cleared his mind and picked a tree to look at.

The light grew dimmer, and the trees started to move and shift. Saplings sprung from the ground and larger trees withered, fell, and crumbled to mulch. Joshua pulled himself out of meditation and marveled at what he had just beheld.

He would often pass times of wakefulness reading the literature of Earth contained on the servers. He read much of what were considered "classics" by English contemporaries of their day. He appreciated Shakespeare's plays for their wit. He could see the appeal in Charles Dickens' character-driven stories. He enjoyed the optimism of Jane Austen's romantic novels, the childhood jaunts found in Mark Twain's writings, the slow suspense of Stephen King, the honest, smart dialogue of Orson Scott Card, and the serious themes in the fantasy settings of J.K. Rowling. He recognized authors for their original thoughts, as Mary Shelley demonstrated in coming up with Frankenstein's monster, and when Bram Stoker created Dracula (well, maybe he borrowed a *bit* from Vlad the Impaler). There were many variations on these stories later on, but they often paled in comparison with the originals.

Joshua noticed many of these stories would posit theories to a question humanity struggled to find a definitive answer to, including him: What is the nature of the human soul?

Does a part of me really continue on after my body dies, or am I just the sum of my physical parts?

To this he could find no definitive answer. His father had made him familiar with the Holy Bible during his upbringing, and he recognized the faith his father had in the assurances of an afterlife as just that; faith. There was no way any person could know of a *surety* without experiencing death for themselves. There were many "out-of-body" experiences recorded in scientific case-studies, but many people attributed these experiences to random firings of the brain synapses. There was no plausible way to create a falsifiable experiment in order to test whether a soul really existed outside of the body; at least no way that didn't involve people willfully being killed and brought back. And even if they did, how would science record the outcome with any meaning beyond "someone else's experience?" Evidence was a problem.

The evidence (or lack thereof) *he* had before him seemed to indicate there *was* no "soul." Even though *Frankenstein* was a work of fiction—it wasn't likely sentient life could be reanimated even if *all* the parts of a body were perfectly in place—he and the rest of his generation were "built," in a similar manner. At what point in his creation did his father "inject" his soul?

It was confusing to Joshua how his father—the same man who taught him the importance of the scientific study of the observable universe—could hold on to unfalsifiable claims so rigidly.

There was no test he was aware of that could be performed to prove the existence of a God either. His father must have adopted his belief in a creator due to the fact that he had a choice to make in the face of tragedy. He could: 1. Believe it's part of the plan set out by an all-

powerful deity and that it would be for his ultimate good,
2. Believe there *was* a deity, but become angry with him due
to unfairness, or 3. Abandon all belief in deity and attribute
all tragedy to chance or human cruelty.

In the light of this understanding, Joshua could see
why his father might choose to believe in a God with a
plan. It certainly saved him from a life of bitterness or
carelessness as to the consequences of his actions. But still,
it nagged at Joshua how a learned man such as his father
could knowingly make a choice such as that, when there
was no way to collect evidence in support of it.

Joshua had read many debates that took place on
Earth's archived forums concerning evolution vs.
creationism. People from both sides took part in heated,
passionate debates about how one side seemed to disprove
the other. Those on the side of science argued that all of
the evidence collected in favor of evolution was
indisputable, and took place over millions of years,
according to carbon dating. Joshua agreed within himself
that the burden of proof lay on the creationists to present
evidence to counter the theory of evolution, but in that
same sense, the scientific community didn't even claim to
have the ability to disprove the existence of a divine
creator, according to their own rules.

It came down to this for him: The religious had no

observable evidence of their own lending credibility to their theories outside of "it is written." (At least no evidences that could be replicated under the conditions of an experiment.) So his hands were tied. Joshua decided to put aside "belief" in exchange for "observable evidence," none of which led him to believe in a creator or a soul.

Still, every once in a while Joshua would find himself speaking aloud, in case his father *did* still exist in some form and was listening. Since science could only "disprove" and not "prove" anything, Joshua had to allow for the chance that someday his current stance on the soul could be disproven. Joshua had to admit to himself, he didn't *know,* so there was always the possibility he was wrong.

One waking hour, Joshua went down to the rec room and sat at the piano. He then played Rachmaninov's Prelude in G Minor, note-for-note, just as his father had watched him do when he was eleven. The landscape of the composition raced through his mind in a blanket of glorious color. He found the octaves much easier to play now that his hands were larger, but it was still the same driving song until the middle section. Then it became a cascade of notes with a sweet melody dancing atop the flurry. The line repeated, and Joshua noticed a lower melody echoing the upper one. It felt as if the mournful notes were climbing upward, longing to escape the minor key they were imprisoned in, hovering on the verge of breaking through into a bright major key and fluttering away, when stealthily, the driving chords recaptured them and refused to let them escape its growing fury. Despite the fact that it was him who played through the piece, Joshua was still amazed at the powerful sounds he was making come from the instrument, and how they seemed to connect to every emotion he was feeling. When the last notes echoed through the cavernous room and faded, he straightened up and wiped the sweat from his brow. The experience was so familiar, he turned around on the bench, expecting to see his father looking at him, smiling with pride.

Nobody was there.

When one year of voyage remained, several technicians were awakened by the computer systems. Joshua watched them from his places of hiding as they prepped the ship for The Elites' awakening. The seeds in the nurseries had to be reawakened and planted for food and potential inclusion in (or takeover of) a new ecosystem. A sharp pain pierced Joshua's heart as he watched them do the job Darrell should have been doing.

The technicians noticed evidences of aging in the chambers Joshua had stayed in, and he overheard them attributing it to "faulty life-support systems." Fortunately, Joshua's presence would remain hidden for the time being. Nevertheless, Joshua made it a point to shadow their movements so he could learn more about the plan when they reached the planet.

Of course, he or they couldn't *really* know what this new world would hold: It was entirely possible that the planet was uninhabitable and they were all doomed to run out of time, blindly searching for another option. Humanity's decision to cast off toward this particular planet was the best educated guess they could make, but the fact remained; it *was* still just a guess. As vast as this universe was, he wondered just how many survival missions to other planets ended up with a casket of "survivors" floating aimlessly through space because of a wrong guess. It was a grim thought, but it stared him in the face the closer they got to their destination.

By staying within earshot, Joshua learned that in the remaining year, the ship would slowly decelerate out of light speed until it was about one month away from the planet at cruising speed.

They needed to be able to halt their progress and observe the planet from a distance before trying to land on it. This made logical sense to Joshua: If the planet was water-based and could sustain life, there always remained the chance that intelligent life had evolved as well.

Which brought them to the hangar: Inside the massive hangar, tens of thousands of drone ships hung from the ceiling, each armed with weaponry and able to be controlled from here by the hundreds by a single person. The larger, manned gunships docked on the floor of the hangar, ready to roll out when the floor opened, followed by the smaller, hanging drones. Toward the back wall were a few dozen observation pods, specifically designed to be deployed to the planet and act as bases of operations and laboratories for a small group of scientists. Near those were slightly larger personnel carriers. There were bay doors around the side walls for individual ship deployment, but the design of the floor made it possible for all of the ships to be deployed quickly. It was apparent the people of Earth had prepared for any contingency, including that of attack. Joshua watched from the vents as technicians checked weapons and flight systems in ship after ship.

To his dismay, Joshua noticed the warships outnumbered the peace-mission-specific ones, one hundred-to-one. Were the people of Earth showing their inclination toward a preemptive strike, or were they just over-preparing in case of a hostile reception?

Regardless, Joshua knew he didn't want to be involved in whatever course they took, and he continued planning his "escape" when the rest of the ship's passengers were awoken. He prepared an observation pod to take him to the planet's surface when they were in the pod's range. He chose a pod directly in front of a bay door, which he had programmed to open when he commanded it to and expose the force field leading to space without alerting the ship it had been opened. He only hoped he could get a big enough head start when he launched so he could make it to the planet's surface before he was observed and pursued. He was under no illusions that his existence was not supposed to be, according to the Speaker and the Council.

The observation pod was equipped with supply storage, a laboratory, a kitchenette and sleeping quarters for a crew of five. He hated taking resources away from the scientists who would be in need of them, but he couldn't fathom stealthily sneaking a gigantic gunship out, and the drones were severely lacking for cockpit space.

So it was this pod he familiarized himself intimately with. He studied the schematics of each system so he could perform any needed maintenance in times of trouble, and he memorized the flight manual and reentry procedures, immediately giving himself the motor skills pilots developed over years of flight school.

For the next few months, Joshua crept around the main ship collecting food rations, sensory equipment, medical supplies and other survival gear and stowed them away on his pod, all the while escaping the notice of the forward party of technicians. He logged into the main system and kept abreast of their list of items to accomplish, so he could hide in a section of the ship apart from the busywork they conducted. He toyed with the idea of playing with them, like leaving cryptic messages for them to find, as if voices from the void of space were calling out for revenge, but ultimately he decided it would not benefit him if they concluded someone else was awake on the ship. He would just have to settle for playing out their most outrageous reactions in his head.

Joshua tried to plan for every scenario that could play out between then and the time he launched. He studied every scientific journal relating to terraforming theory, and downloaded many more journals to the pod's database for further study, due to time constraints. He uploaded as many applications and as much pertinent information as he could foresee needing in the future, filling as many external hard drives as he dared "borrow" from other parts of the ship. He maximized his time left by "sleeping" for about one minute, which was about 6 hours of real time. He didn't dare sleep longer, for fear of being discovered by the technicians now patrolling the ship. Of course, all of his planning and preparations would be for naught if the planet proved uninhabitable, but he prepared anyway, just in case. Humanity had gone to great lengths to predict the greatest possibility of a match to Earth, even going so far as eliminating planets hundreds of light years closer due to the slightest doubts. It was interesting to note that even though science discounted faith as a valid tool of measurement, faith was ultimately what set them on the course they were on now. In the absence of knowing, believing was the second best option.

So said everyone faced with their impending death.

10

The survivors of Earth were awoken and their vitals were taken. When they were cleared, they were injected with hormones to help their muscles overcome atrophy and taken to their rooms to rejuvenate. The time was drawing near.

After 490 years of traveling at the speed of light, Keppler-186f was visible. The ship had slowed down to cruising speed so the telescope could focus on the light being bounced off the planet's surface. Images of the planet were projected to the survivors' individual rooms. Cheering echoed down every corridor as they saw images of water, land, clouds, and climes. Except for the shape of only one massive continent, it was as if they were seeing Earth again.

Council Speaker Salman bin Sultan felt his heart leap in his chest. Here was a world of new opportunity, waiting for someone to lay claim to its precious resources. He had a blank canvas in front of him; a fresh, new start to build a world the way he saw fit. He had spent an entire lifetime on Earth shaping his life according to other men's rules, and now here he was in front of a giant reset button.

He counted himself fortunate that the connections he built in his former life were the very connections he needed when the meteor appeared in the night sky.

Salman was of the Royal Saudi family on Earth, he had many opportunities placed in front of him by virtue of his family's money and influence. He earned a master's degree from an Ivy League University in the United States, and there became fluent in English, politics and economics, and was introduced to many future world leaders. His appointments as Vice Minister of Defence and Aviation and later Minister of Foreign Affairs gave him worldwide connections, and he became part of the globalist movement operating in the shadows of legitimate governments.

Although he officially worked under the direction of his uncle, the King of Saudi Arabia, he was privy to a lot more information than his dear uncle was. Not only that, but he had access to oil money, which helped him earn many friends and favors from others around the world.

When it became apparent that the world was going to meet its end, Salman invested in the only resource that made any sense as far as survival was concerned; scientists. After he became the new King, Salman suggested to his fellow world leaders that they form a coalition council in Riyadh consisting of the greatest minds in every scientific

field in order to create their own salvation (it was apparent
to Salman that Allah was not going to step in). But in his
official capacity as King, he made sure to invoke Allah's
name on every broadcast, in order to keep the support
from the hopeful believers in the region. There were many
who had taken the opportunity to gather under a false
prophet who led them to their demise while attacking a
very prepared Israel. These opportunists did much for his
making a case to the scientific council for pursuing a
"peaceful" solution, and with his state-controlled media
and new international military muscle, he succeeded in
keeping their discussions secret from most of the world.

The other members of the shadow government
were present at the summit and they formulated a plan of
their own after the scientists decided on the plan to escape
Earth in a gigantic ship. Thousands of the best engineers
and builders were brought on in order to build the vessel,
using their newly-formed military coalition for protection
and secrecy. Near the end of the frenzied build, those in his
shadow council started gathering their families to the
region, unbeknownst to everyone else.

Salman's former connections to the military, and
the masses of devout followers gave him the upper hand
when the plan was put into action. The world's elite forces
under his and his fellow world leaders' command bought

passage by silencing with deadly precision the builders, engineers, and others who knew about the ship. Only those whom The Council deemed necessary for survival were invited—or compelled—to ride along. This involved about one thousand people, but only his Council had any say in who these passengers would be. Space was limited, and hard decisions *had* to be made. Unfortunately, the scientists' families, as well as his dear departed uncle, the former King of Saudi Arabia, didn't make the list.

Salman paused from his recollection and looked now upon the reasons he justified his inhumane actions; his granddaughters. His daughter and son-in-law shared a suite with Salman and his wife, along with their three girls. The girls were now sitting on the floor watching the screen and speculating about what type of animals might live on the planet.

"What if there's a cross between an elephant and a giraffe?" Fatima said.

"It probably could only lift its head off the ground once a day," Malika replied. "What would be the purpose for an animal like that?"

"What's an elf-ant?" asked Aiesha. She had been born on the ship, and at the age of seven, wasn't aware of many of the creatures her teen sisters knew.

"El-*AH*-phant," Malika corrected. "It was the

largest land mammal on Earth. It had a head about the size of your bed and a big…"

"Mammal?" Aisha asked sincerely. Fatima laughed when Malika looked back at her mother, exasperated.

"You know, it probably won't matter if I describe it to you anyway," Malika said. "The animals there will probably be like nothing we've ever seen."

"Maybe we'll have to live with big-headed aliens," Fatima said.

"I already do," Malika replied. Now it was Aisha's turn to laugh.

The sound of her laughter brought a smile to Salman's face. He envisioned a world where his granddaughters would not have to live under the strict rule of sharia law. Where they could learn, choose a husband, and rule when he and his son had passed on. With religion guiding most of the tenets of sharia, this could be abolished in light of the absence of Allah in their salvation. At least according to him. There would be some who would want to cling to the traditions of the old world, but Salman had plans for them to have limited power when they landed. He knew enough of politics to create a need for his leadership, and he already had a head start as the Council Speaker.

Besides, he didn't trust anyone else to be able to

make the hard decisions he had been faced with.

Sleep came heavy to Salman's eyes and he drifted off.

"Sir, wake up."

Salman opened his eyes and saw his most trusted guard standing above him. "Sir, there's an issue," Sayid said. "We need you to come with us."

Salman put on a robe and followed the SF guards down to the flight deck. The captain noticed him come in and motioned for him to have a seat.

"Thank you for coming down," Captain Lamb said. "There's been a development we thought you should know about and share with the Council." He pulled up an image of the planet on the screen. "There," he said.

Salman looked at the image of the planet and didn't notice anything. "What am I looking for?" he asked.

"Look at the edge of the planet, where the sun is not shining," Captain Lamb said. "Do you see it?"

"Just cut to the point and tell me!" Salman demanded. The captain swallowed hard and pointed to a small, dark area of the planet.

"Lights, sir. There are cities down there."

11

Joshua noticed an increase in activity among members of the Council. From his hiding places, he listened in on a few meetings and learned the planet was inhabited by intelligent life capable of building cities the size of Earth's larger metropolises. Their greatest fears seemed to be confirmed, and plans had to be made. Not only did they fear any scenario they could imagine— especially that of not being welcomed if they came in peace—but they also feared the unknown, like how the intelligent life looked. Deep down, they feared trying to coexist with creatures that might regard humans as second-class citizens or even animals. What quality of life could they expect as strange intruders?

It was apparent from chatter around the ship that an important planning meeting had been held without Joshua being able to listen in. He located Brand working alone in a maintenance corridor and came out of hiding to speak with him.

"Josh!" Brand exclaimed while wrapping him in a tight embrace. "I wasn't sure you were still alive! Did you find an empty cryo-chamber?"

"Not exactly," Joshua replied. "Let's just say I hibernated through the voyage."

"How is that possible? You don't look a day older than when I went to sleep! Well, maybe a *little* older. Look at these guns!" Brand felt the biceps on Joshua's arms.

"It's a long story," Joshua said. "Hey, Brand, I need to know what the Council is planning to do now that they know the planet is inhabited. Are they going to release their armada?"

"Not yet...and hopefully never! They plan on disguising the ship with an increase of speed—something about the way light bends—I don't know; I'm not a physicist. Then they are going to launch a larger drone at the same trajectory when they are hidden behind the planet's moon, so it will burn up harmlessly in the atmosphere while they hide the ship on the dark side of the moon."

"As if the drone were the object in space, continuing its course," Joshua completed the thought out loud to show Brand he understood. "That would help alleviate the fears of any invasion."

"Yeah, and meanwhile, we send out pods on secret observation missions, to scope out conditions on the planet before we make any major moves," Brand said.

"Huh. I guess that's as good a plan as any," Joshua

said. "Let's just hope the aliens aren't advanced enough to find us out."

This information altered Joshua's plans, as well. He had planned to live out the rest of his life alone on the planet, apart from the others, but now he realized this would not be one consolidated group, easy to avoid. There were other inhabitants on the planet he would need to avoid as well, which meant finding less populated ground. He would have to find enough seclusion to plant his Earth-native garden without being discovered, and that meant space away from cities. His survival mission now included the possibility of avoiding being killed.

"Where have you been staying?" Brand asked.

"I spend the majority of my time hidden away in an observation pod. It has comfortable sleeping quarters and it's separated enough from the ship's population to be secluded. Every once in awhile I'll venture out into the maintenance corridors to see what's going on, but it's getting harder to remain undiscovered with everyone awake."

"I'm glad you found me! I've been worried sick about you," Brand said. He gave Joshua another uncomfortable bear hug. Joshua realized Brand needed physical contact to connect with people, and tolerated it. Somewhere in this embrace was a reconnection with a child

Brand had lost.

"I promised your dad I'd keep you safe," Brand said. Then he held Joshua at arms' length and looked him in the eyes. "Do you need me to take you in? I could convince the Council that…"

"They don't want me alive," Joshua said. "I'm witness to their monstrosities and evidence of their failures, and they can't have that. I'm fine, Brand, really. I've made it four hundred seventy-two years so far, and I'm doing great!"

"And you still haven't quite finished puberty!" Brand laughed and punched him painfully in the arm.

―――――――――――

Joshua was preparing plant starts in his pod when he heard voices outside in the hangar. He peeked out the porthole and saw groups of scientists and SF agents approaching the pods. A group of four scientists and one agent broke off and headed directly for his pod. He had to think quickly. He locked the doors to give himself time. Escaping through the top hatch might make noise that would alert others in the hangar, so it would have to be in the pod that he hid. Unfortunately, the pod didn't have the same hiding places as the large ship in order to maximize use of the smaller space. He didn't have time to hide any evidences of his living there, but he figured it was more important to hide himself.

He heard muffled sounds of a code being entered and the door handle being tried. "It's not opening," someone said.

"Try again. Maybe you entered the code wrong."

Joshua came up with a place to hide and set about getting into place while they struggled with the locked door.

"Hey, can we get a maintenance guy down here?" someone yelled.

Joshua put on one of the spacesuits hanging along the wall. These were designed so someone could enter quickly from the back of the suit, after which it sealed tightly up the back. He sealed the helmet to the flange, then flipped the switch on the side of the helmet for the sun shield and the visor went dark. He couldn't see out in the low light, but neither could anyone see in and notice the suit was occupied. Then he stood still in the place where the suit hung, just as the door opened.

"Whoa! It looks like someone's already prepped our shuttle," someone said. "Grant, did you sneak in here and do this?"

"Wasn't me," Grant replied. "Huh. Mysterious!"

Joshua could hear them looking around the shuttle. "Someone's been sleeping in *my* bed," Grant said.

"Must be *just right*," someone else joked.

"Do we have a stowaway on the ship?"

"A five-hundred-year-old stowaway?" Grant said. "Unlikely. Still..."

"Well, whoever it was did us a favor," a female voice said. "Less prep work for us to do before our mission."

"It looks like everything we need is here. The lab is set up, the food rations are in storage... heck, they even started some of your botany projects, Liz!"

"*Some* of them. I'll still have to take some of this equipment." Joshua could hear cases being dropped and scooted along the floor.

He was surprised to hear them act so contented with the situation. They seemed not to worry as much about the mysterious intruder as they were about the work it would take getting ready to launch their secret mission to the planet's surface. They stopped talking and looked around for a bit more. A few times he could hear people very close to where the spacesuits hung. He forced himself to relax and slow his breathing.

"Well, I'm heading back," Grant said.

"You're not going to make your bed first?" Liz said.

"I never make my bed," Grant said. "*You* should know that." Joshua heard the dull thud of a punch and some playful laughter.

"You only wish," Liz said.

"I'm taking off, too." one of the unnamed crewmembers said. "Did anyone get the new code from the maintenance guy?"

"I got it," Liz said.

Their voices got quieter as they exited the ship. Joshua assumed everyone was off the pod and turned off the sun shield so he could make sure, and had *just* dropped his hand back into place as the SF agent who was with them turned around in the doorway for one last look. His gaze settled on the spacesuits for a minute, and Joshua got the impression he might be onto him. As he planned out in his mind what he would do if the agent approached him, the agent turned around and closed the hatch.

Someone's been wearing my spacesuit, and they're still in it! Joshua thought.

12

Touchdown on the moon was mere minutes away. Speaker Salman bin Sultan watched nervously from the flight deck as the captain gave commands to the pilot operating the drone. The drone was launched and brought up to the same speed the ship had been traveling at when they were completely cloaked behind the moon.

"Prepare for touchdown," Captain Lamb commanded.

"Landing gear down," reported one pilot.

"In ten. Easy on the back thrusters! 5-4-3-2-1," Captain Lamb said. The ship rocked as it settled into the dusty surface of a crater. Nobody cheered as Salman had envisioned they would if they had landed on the planet. Instead, the room was filled with a tense silence.

Captain Lamb turned to his crew. "Bring up the drone visuals on monitor one," he ordered. The drone operator's monitor now filled the main screen so everyone in the room could watch. "Slowly angle it toward the planet, as if the planet's gravity is starting to affect it now." The planet came into view on the monitor as the drone adjusted its boosters to turn left. "Angle it so the atmosphere will take a little longer to burn it up," the

Captain ordered.

"It needs to seem like it was a larger object."

"These drones were built to endure entry into atmo," one engineer said, "unless they enter in at the steep angle it might not burn up."

"I'm well aware of that, Craig," Captain Lamb said. "But we don't have to perform a nosedive, here. Just enough to create a slow, steady burn until the drone is gone."

"Are we *sure* they didn't see us land back here?" Salman asked.

"From the angle of the sun behind the planet, the moon is in crescent phase as seen from the planet's surface, Captain Lamb answered. "We had pretty good cover under darkness coming in."

The planet was in full view on the monitor when one of the ensigns noticed something coming from the planet.

"Sir, what is that strange cloud?" he asked. Everyone stared at the spot he pointed out. Captain Lamb's eyes grew wide.

"What is it?" Salman asked him.

"I was an astronaut for NASA on Earth and happened to witness the launch of a Russian ship from the planet's surface when I was deployed to the International Space Station," Captain Lamb said, solemnly. "It looked a lot like that."

"Is it coming for us?" Salman asked.

"It doesn't look like it. Its trajectory looks like it's tracking the drone."

"Are they coming to make contact?" Councilman Xi asked.

"We can't be sure," Captain Lamb said.

"Do you want me to change course and wait for their arrival, sir?" the drone pilot asked.

"Negative," Captain Lamb said. "We don't want to give ourselves away. Just stay on course and let's see how this plays out."

Salman looked around the room and was relieved to see he wasn't the only one who might look worried. He tried to control the emotion on his face, so the others would know he was still in charge.

"If they try to make contact, I would be happy to try to communicate with them," Salman said.

"Let's not worry about that *just* yet," Captain Lamb said. Then added, a little late for Salman's satisfaction, "sir."

They all watched the monitor for the next twenty

or so minutes, as the cloud turned into an object traveling through space. They adjusted the camera on the drone so the object was centered in the monitor. From the front, Salman couldn't make out any details of the object steadily growing larger. It was apparent the object was set to intercept the drone, and would probably do so before the drone reached the atmosphere.

"It doesn't seem to be slowing down, sir," the pilot told Captain Lamb.

"No, it doesn't," confirmed the captain. "It looks to be on a collision course."

"Evasive maneuvers?"

"Negative. Stay your course."

They all watched in shock as the object ran into the drone and the monitor went static.

Cameras outside of the main ship captured a soundless explosion that obliterated the drone and the object that had been launched from the planet. The blindingly bright light at the center of the explosion indicated the launched object had been created with the ability to consume space debris in an oxygen-free environment.

"A missile," Captain Lamb said.

"So much for a warm welcome," Salman said.

13

"Joshua, are you in there? It's Brand. Open up if you're in there."

Joshua got up from his desk and opened the pod door. Outside on the ramp stood a very concerned-looking Brand. "Come in," Joshua beckoned, and he closed and locked the door behind both of them. "What's going on?"

Brand filled Joshua in on how the drone had been destroyed. Brand was on the flight deck and witnessed the incident firsthand.

"So, what do they plan on doing now?" Joshua asked.

"I think the Speaker saw this as a sign of aggression. He's talking about a devastating pre-emptive strike to each major city. EMPs, nukes, everything we can throw at them."

"Before we even try to make contact?"

"That's what he's worried about. If we make contact and let them know we're here, that takes away the element of surprise."

"How can he consider this? We have no idea what these aliens are capable of! What sorts of advanced weaponry they have, what defenses they... first of all, we can't even be sure they really *are* aggressors! That missile could have been launched by someone acting alone on the planet!"

Joshua was letting his emotions take control. *This was just like the Speaker, eliminating anyone that stands in the way of his ambitions!*

"The missile came from just outside a large city. Most likely a capital."

"We can't do this! Millions of their kind will die, or more likely, we'll all be killed trying!"

"What other choice do we have?" Brand asked. "We can't sit up here forever and it's too late to turn around and find another option. We have to get down *there*!"

"They outnumber us, millions-to-one!"

"But we have the higher ground," Brand said. "And that's why the Council is considering the Speaker's surprise attack. We'll launch the EMPs, which will disrupt their communications enough to throw their forces out of sync, not to mention grounding any electronic equipment they might have. We pick off any spots of resistance they might show from up here with precision nukes, then allow the lack of power to do most of the killing for us."

"Us?" Joshua asked, tears welling up in his eyes.

"Come on, Josh," Brand put a hand on his shoulder. "It's not like I love the idea… it's just that I see no other option. Any observation pod we send out for reconnaissance will be blown to bits. It's them or us, and I like *us*!"

"We don't even know who *they* are," Joshua said.

Joshua had to get Darrell's time capsule. He knew it wasn't vital, but to him it was a connection to his former life, and he had plans for a new one. He traversed the length of the spacious hangar in the maintenance catwalks suspended from the ceiling, so he wouldn't be spotted by the crews now readying the gunships below. It was amazing to him how even *pilots* neglected to look up. He passed completely unaware to the masses of people below. Before he left the room, he changed the gravity settings on the wall console just slightly.

He made his way through the entire ship through the maintenance corridors, but had to dart through the main hall to cross the gap between the main part of the ship and the Elite's quarters. He glanced quickly at the entry pad and noticed the code pattern had changed since he last came through, but it only took a moment for him to eliminate the most unlikely movements in his head and decode it. He slipped in and quickly hid behind the panel, collecting the capsule from its hiding place.

From the ship's intercom came a voice: "All flight personnel, please report to the hangar for final preparations."

Time was running short. Joshua climbed out of the panel and replaced it, then went to open the door to the main corridor, when it was opened from the other side. Joshua found himself staring directly into the startled face of Speaker Salman bin Sultan. Standing behind him were four large SF agents. Joshua figured his best chance was to play it off casually and hope the Speaker didn't recognize him as the same genetically-modified boy he had given so many awards to.

"Pardon, me, sir," Joshua said as he brushed past them and continued down the corridor toward his escape behind the next maintenance hatch. He could feel the Speaker's eyes boring holes into his back. His shocked expression had been the same as someone's who might have seen a ghost.

"Stop!" the Speaker commanded.

Joshua pretended not to hear. The hatch was only 10 feet away.

"Get him!"

Joshua broke into a run and made it through the

hatch with the sounds of footsteps close behind. He knew if they followed him into the maintenance corridors, he would have the advantage, having explored the labyrinthine passages in his youth. Sure enough, two of them followed.

"All SF, be on the alert for a dark-haired teen dressed in a flight suit in maintenance corridor four! His capture is priority one!" an agent behind him radioed.

The map of the ship unfolded before Joshua's mind and he quickly assessed the probabilities of capture. He tracked in his head the probable routes of the two agents who stayed in the main corridor, and where they would be able to successfully cut him off running at a sprint. He instantly eliminated five of his possible escape routes. Now he turned his full attention to escaping the guards behind him.

Up ahead was a caged ladder that led up to a catwalk. Joshua scrambled up the ladder, feeling the metal bars rub against his back and figuring it would be a tighter squeeze for the larger men. He reached the catwalk above just as the agents were entering the caged ladder. Joshua made as if he were going to keep running down the catwalk, but when the agents had struggled halfway up the ladder, he climbed over the guard rail, jumped back down to the main corridor, and began to pry the vent cover off a large duct. Joshua knew this would take a few moments of precious time, but he had bought time with his path.

"Go down!" the agent highest up on the ladder yelled. The cage around the ladder prevented them from just jumping off the ladder, so they began the labored climb down, grunting and huffing angrily.

Joshua finished prying the cover off and climbed head-first into the duct. He knew he had to make his way through the engine room in order to get to the main ventilation chamber. This duct led to the engine room. He low crawled his way through the vent and started hearing noises behind him as he neared the opening at the far end. His pursuers must have finally gotten free of the ladder.

The cylindrical engine room was humming loudly as the photon engines converted collected starlight to physical movement. Joshua was barely aware of how the process worked, but he knew the light in the central chamber was actually dense in a tangible way. The engine used the physical properties of light in the mirrored central chamber to propel the ship through space. As Brand had once explained to him, "It basically made a giant laser to push the ship against."

The sounds of the pursuers behind him let him know he had to act quickly to impede their progress. He ran to the central light chamber and looked for a retaining bolt at the same height as the vent through which he had crawled. He pulled a crescent wrench from his pocket that he had swiped from Brand's tool belt earlier.

"Sorry, Brand," Joshua whispered to nobody. He removed the bolt and a harsh beam of light shot in a direct line into the vent behind him.

"Ow, ow! Go back, go back!" a voice shouted from the vent. "Hurry, before I catch fire!" Joshua smiled, but his smile didn't last.

"There he is!" shouted another voice from a ledge above him which followed the circular walls. Two more SF agents had entered the engine room through the main door and were standing between Joshua and his escape to the main ventilation chamber. Getting around them was going to be tricky.

One of them radioed their location to others, and they set about climbing down both ladders in order to box Joshua in. Joshua knew he had to move quickly before any others arrived. In his head, he adjusted the routes of the most likely responders and gave himself a timer: 45 seconds.

Joshua grabbed the chrome-plated crescent wrench and, bracing his hand against a railing, reflected the beam toward the nearest agent. It pushed his hand against the railing with a powerful force, but visibly affected the agent. He started climbing back up to escape the intense light. He got back up onto the catwalk and started going toward the other ladder.

41 seconds.

"The beam is gone, let's go!" Joshua heard the first agent yell in the vent. Unfortunately for him, the wrench was starting to superheat, and Joshua had to drop it so he wouldn't burn his hand any further. The beam went back into the vent.

"Ow! Go back! Go back, dammit!"

36 seconds.

He noticed the farthest agent in the engine room had reached the bottom of the ladder and was running toward him. Joshua made a decision in an instant and jumped onto the nearest ladder, climbing upward. The agent on the ledge above him ran back to Joshua's ladder and started to climb down. As he drew close, Joshua spun onto the back of the ladder and grabbed the bottommost foot of the agent, pulling toward him sharply. Rather than let his leg break, the agent chose to let go with his hands and fall backward, catching himself with his knee bent behind the ladder rung.

28 seconds.

Joshua quickly reached around the hanging agent and unclasped his web belt, then wrapped it around the ladder *and* the agent's waist, clasping it on backward so it would be hard for him to undo. Once he was immobilized upside-down, Joshua climbed up the ladder a bit, then came around to the front of it, making sure to plant a boot firmly on the agent's groin as he ascended the rest of the way.

19 seconds.

He ran toward the main door to try to prop it shut. A laser pulse hit the bulkhead near his face. Joshua fell to the ledge floor and lay as flat as he could.

"Are you *crazy*?" he yelled down. "If a shot hits the photon engines, we'll all die!"

14 seconds.

He could hear running footsteps coming from the open door. He had to act quickly or this escape act would get a lot more complicated.

Here's hoping the agent has any logic to appeal to! Joshua thought. He stood up and ran toward the door, half expecting to be shot at again. Fortunately, the agent had put his weapon away and was trying to help his comrade off the ladder.

9 seconds.

He could hear the footsteps of four men running down the maintenance corridor toward the engine room.

8...

7...

Another shot scorched the catwalk below him. Joshua jumped against the wall. *Was this guy serious?*

4...

3...

He had no choice but to run for the door. He could hear commands coming through the door as if they were already there. He gritted his teeth and ran the last few steps.

2...

"Don't shoot!" someone yelled. It must have been enough coming from someone besides Joshua, because no shots were fired.

1...

Joshua reached the door and slammed it shut, making sure the agents didn't see it was he who was right behind the door. He took the bolt from the engine wall and jammed it tightly into the gap between the door and the threshold, kicking it into place with his boot. The broad head of the bolt nestled snugly in a gap in the ledge floor, effectively locking the door. The agents' muffled voices and pounding could be heard on the outside of the door. "Is he still in the engine room?" a garbled voice asked over the radio.

"Affirmative," the agent in the room answered.

The agent below him had succeeded in freeing his friend from the ladder and the two of them were now climbing back up to Joshua. He had a few more moments to run over to another vent cover and pry it open. He knew this was where he needed to get to in order to keep the SF guessing. As the agents got to the top of the ladder, Joshua dove into the duct.

The duct sloped steeply downward, and Joshua let himself slide as quickly as possible. He heard a noise growing louder up ahead and when he saw the opening at the other end, he pressed his forearms and feet against the sides of the duct to slow his momentum. He barely screeched to a full stop before falling to certain death.

The duct opened to the large, cylindrical ventilation chamber. The giant blades spun menacingly below and they noisily pushed recycled air up through the now opened ducts all along the walls.

He reached out and grabbed a ladder to his right, pulling himself out to stand on the rungs.

"Can we get maintenance to tell us where 'ACS-14' leads?" Joshua heard one of the agents following him radio from up the duct. Joshua paused to listen for an insight into their plan.

"To the atmosphere circulation hub," someone radioed back.

"And from there, where?"

"Everywhere," came the response.

"Great!"

"But I wouldn't recommend going in there," the voice warned.

But by the time those words had been spoken, it was too late. One agent had jumped in, and was sliding rapidly toward the hub. Joshua climbed up the ladder and clenched his eyes tightly when he heard the man fly into the hub and fall screaming into the spinning blades.

"Rory?!" the remaining agent called down the hatch.

"RORY!"

Joshua just kept climbing, never looking down at the carnage below. The wind blew the gruesome smell of death up to his nostrils, and he had to focus on the map in his head to keep from passing out.

He hopped over to the next ladder and listened in on a duct leading to the hangar. "You stand guard here! If anyone comes out, you're authorized to use deadly force."

"Are we authorized to shoot?"

"No guns! There's too much ordinance in here."

One set of footsteps going away.

The SF agents were guarding his exit route through the hangar. He ascertained with the radio announcement of where he was, they would now be guarding every vent leading from this room. There was one path they *wouldn't* be guarding, though, and it was in this that Joshua climbed. He knew this was backtracking, but for now it seemed his only option.

Joshua climbed to the top and entered the forested oxygen room.

The room was dark once again, and his eyes had to adjust to starlight for him to proceed through the trees. He looked for a tree with thick enough foliage to conceal him until he could figure out a plan.

"I know you're here."

A voice rang out from the darkness, echoing off the clear ceiling above. Joshua quickly ducked behind a tree. He recognized the voice as Speaker Salman bin Sultan.

"There's no point in running. Every exit from here is guarded. I have authorized my Special Forces to kill you when they see you."

Joshua peeked out from behind the tree and tried to see where the Speaker stood. In all the shadows of the trees, it was impossible to tell where he was unless he moved. Joshua decided to use that knowledge to his own advantage as well. He settled back behind the tree and held still. Unfortunately, the tree he chose was away from any others which could provide cover in a getaway.

"You might not think it, but I remember you, Joshua Hawker. You excelled in research more than any other child from the Darwin Generation. We had great hopes for the future when we witnessed what you could do.

"Do you want to know how I got here? On this ship, I mean. Of all the billions of people on Earth, *I* got a coveted golden ticket to survive.

"Well, that's just it, I guess. I gave away the answer with the question. I'm a survivor.

"I had a revelation when the meteorite struck and doomed all humanity to extinction: There is *no* god. If there is no god, then there is no such thing as good or evil. Just *being*. Just action and reaction. Nobody judging my actions.

"If I end someone else's life to extend my own, I have just accomplished something humanity's 'god' could not. The universe pronounced a death sentence on the human race, and 'god' was powerless to save them.

"So I took matters into my own hands. I became more of a god to humanity than the one they had before. I built a lifeboat to escape our sinking ship. I rescued the human race! Right now, we are all that's left of planet Earth. Think about that.

"You shouldn't take it so personally that I jettisoned your friends. I was only doing what I have done my whole life; guaranteeing my survival. There just wasn't enough room or resources to keep you all on. Believe me, if the cryo-chambers did not work in the trial runs, not only would you be dead, but so would all of us by now. You see, I am *still* in the business of being a savior to humankind."

Joshua tried to quiet his breathing when he noticed his heart was beating harder.

"You should be thanking me, even though you will not be around to live on our new home planet. But *humanity* will live on, and your name will be recorded in the history books as one who made the ultimate sacrifice to make this possible!

"Before you cease to exist, I give you this gift.

"Move in."

Joshua could hear footsteps carefully creeping toward him from four directions. Their pace never wavered, so Joshua assumed those approaching him were wearing night-vision goggles. A timer in his head gave him about 10 seconds before they were close enough to shoot him without risking a breach in the ship. If he could just buy two more minutes...

He turned and scrambled up the tree trunk behind him. The quiet hiss of a radio told him they were communicating, but he couldn't hear their whispered conversations. But he could ascertain that they wouldn't shoot now until they could clearly see him in the tree's foliage. Even then, they might not take the shot for fear of hitting the clear ceiling.

He heard their pace quicken. They didn't try to mask their movement now.

Joshua remembered how the light dimmed when he went into time-sleep in this room. He knew it was just a result of the light cycle turning off and on at timed intervals, and his brain retaining the light images long enough to still see. He had been going into stasis for long enough that he knew exactly how long each session lasted in real-time. That was how he came up with a number in his head.

Just one more minute…

"Salman?" Joshua called out.

The footsteps stopped for a second.

"Don't let him stall his demise!" Salman shouted. The footsteps resumed.

Joshua kept talking: "You're the worst of humanity! If you're going to be all that's left, the universe would be better off without us."

"So says the dead boy."

"Nobody *deserves* to die. No one life is more

valuable than another. Might *does not* make right!"

Joshua moved a little higher up the tree so his view of the ground was obstructed. He started to inch out onto a branch. He had to time this just right…

"Actually, it does. I will survive you, and my story will be the only one anybody hears. I win by forfeit."

The SF agents were now gathered at the base of the tree. Joshua could see red lasers flitting through the leaves as they searched for him. He tensed his muscles and prepared to move.

"You're wrong, Salman…" he said. The lasers all honed into his location and he moved his head so he stared directly into them, dilating his pupils.

Now!

He scampered out onto the end of the branch and exposed himself to a clean shot.

"I have *already* survived you by over 400 years!"

The lights of the room turned on and filled the area with daylight. The SF agents beneath him shrieked and tried to pull the night-vision goggles off their heads, and it was in this moment that Joshua jumped down from the tree and sprinted for the vent he had come in from. He dove in before he even heard any sounds of pursuit.

14

Joshua pulled out Darrell's capsule and opened it. The model ship fell from his grasp and a small clanking noise told him it had been destroyed in the whirling blades below. Joshua grabbed the rubber ball and climbed over to a duct two places adjacent. He saw the duct curved sharply to the right, which would suit his purpose well. He threw the rubber ball down the duct so it bounced off as many surfaces as he could make it.

"Over here!" someone shouted. Joshua quickly made his way back to the other duct and began silently crawling toward the vent cover. There were no boots visible outside the opening, so the guard must have responded to his decoy. Joshua looked out the vent across the great hangar to his goal. There was a lot of ground to cover, and there were many guards along this wall watching vent openings.

Joshua took a deep breath and steeled himself for his next move. He turned over onto his back and cocked his knees in front of the gate.

It's now or never, Joshua!

One last breath and Joshua kicked the cover off

the vent. He climbed out as quickly as he could, and saw agents approaching him from all sides. He acted lightning fast, and dropped the nearest guard with a slap to the side of the neck. His swift attack caught the other agents off-guard, and Joshua used their hesitation to start to cut a swath toward his destination.

He unleashed his specialized training on those directly in his path. Broken elbow when one threw a haymaker punch, broken knee when the next prepared for an upper-body attack, dodge, punch, chop the windpipe, run straight through the next one with a forehead to the solar plexus. No wasted movement, and quick immobilizations.

An agent to his left grabbed Joshua's flight suit and Joshua changed his momentum *into* the agent and twisted his body swiftly so the agent's fingers were caught up in the fabric and his wrist broken. His movement backward allowed another agent to grab him from behind in a rear naked choke, and he started to squeeze. The pressure was intense, and Joshua felt himself start to get dizzy.

Joshua reached behind him and pinched the agent on the inside of the thigh. The sudden sharp pain shocked the agent enough to break through his adrenaline and cause him to release his grip. Joshua held onto the man's arm and used it to pull both of his feet up and kick the chest of man facing him. He sprang backward, releasing the man's arm at the same time and creating separation from him with a backward dive roll.

He landed on his feet and saw three men standing in his way. Lightning fast, he sized up their expressions and body language. One stood back a step, and one's eyes darted from Joshua to the man standing at the forefront, who stood in a trained fighter's stance. Instantly, Joshua calculated six different outcomes contingent on his next move, and he went straight for the most dangerous-looking one. He made as if he was going to shoot for his legs, and the trained fighter sprawled backward in anticipation. What he didn't know was that Joshua had predicted this reaction and he jumped upward sharply, knocking him out cold when the crown of his head connected with his chin. The other two, seeing their champion fall, backed off slightly. Joshua took advantage of this opening and sprinted toward his goal.

The agents he hadn't incapacitated chased him, but their larger masses combined with the increased gravity Joshua had set up made it difficult for them to keep up. His legs were used to the higher gravity pull, and the gap between him and the SF agents increased with every step.

They shouted for some of the pilots to help them apprehend Joshua, but those who witnessed Joshua's fighting didn't look too excited to get involved. Some made a half-hearted effort to stand in front of him with their arms outstretched, as if he were an animal to be corralled, but he put his head down and sprinted directly at the smallest pilot with no signs of slowing down. He fixed his eyes on the pilot's eyes and started yelling steadily. It had the intended psychological effect: When Joshua was about three feet from barreling through the pilot, the pilot jumped to the side with his hands up and let him pass, untouched. A few of the pilots took up pursuit, but Joshua still had the advantage.

Someone shouted, "Don't shoot!" and Joshua swerved behind a gunship loaded with explosives. This was enough to remind anyone about the danger of firing a laser in his direction, and no shots were fired.

By the time he reached his pod, he had at least a ten-second lead on everyone chasing him.

Joshua quickly opened the hatch and sat in the cockpit. He fired up the engine and opened the bay door, exposing the force field. He tilted the yoke forward and the pod took off through the force field, leaving his pursuers in a wake of heat.

He looked at his rear monitor, and smiled as he saw a winded agent bend and pick up the small gift he had left behind for the team of scientists whose shuttle he took.

A forget-me-not.

15

"He's going to give us away!" Salman watched the monitor as the pod headed toward the planet's surface.

He was furious! The incompetence of the SF had put his whole plan in jeopardy, and everything was about to be upended by someone who, by all accounts, should be dead! If they were unable to kill him when they jettisoned the Darwin generation, the time he spent out of stasis should have done the job.

How?

"Should we fire, sir?" a crewman asked.

"Yes," Salman ordered. "Send him to his maker."

"Hold on, ensign," Captain Lamb said. It was infuriating to Salman that his command should be superseded by someone who ranked lower than he. "Why don't we wait it out and see what the aliens do."

"He'll expose us!" Salman yelled.

"With all due respect, sir, they might take care of him for us and give us more information about them. For all they know, the kid's ship could be the last of the vessels in their sky. If *we* fire on him, they'll know better. Plus, we'll give away our location."

Salman thought about it. The Captain made a good point, but he still couldn't stand the fact that the crewmembers were more loyal to the captain than he.

"Very well. Let's see how this plays out," Salman said. "It might be more satisfying watching him get destroyed by the very creatures he's running to, anyway."

They continued watching, each crewmember instructed to monitor the planet's surface for signs of a missile launch. Well after the time the drone had been destroyed before, the kid's pod continued flying with no sign of being shot down. He was nearing the atmosphere.

"Where's the missile?" Salman demanded.

"I'm not sure, sir," Captain Lamb said. "It appears they're not going to shoot it down. At least not now." Sayid came in and passed a message to Salman.

"Do you want us to send a pursuit ship?" Captain Lamb asked Salman.

Salman finished reading the message. "No, captain," Salman said. "He'll be taken care of. I've got an inside man. Call off the air strike."

—————————————————

Joshua felt a gun press against the back of his head.

"It wasn't hard to figure out where you'd end up when the call went out," a voice said.

Joshua looked at the reflection cast on the glass by the dim console light. He saw a man dressed in a spacesuit. He now knew why he didn't notice the man when he entered the shuttle, and he also knew the identity of the man.

"Sorry for stealing your ride," Joshua said.

"Turn the ship around or I kill you," the man said.

"No you won't."

"Try me."

"You've already been tried," Joshua said. "I heard the kill order on the main ship. You should have killed me already, but you haven't. My guess is you don't know how to fly. You need me alive."

"The Speaker gave the command, and I'll do it even if it means my death."

"Okay, then. Shoot." Joshua waited. He guessed any person who hadn't been *forced* to be on the ship had a strong survival instinct.

"Turn the shuttle around!" the agent demanded.

"Do you have a name?" Joshua asked. "We might as well get to know one another better. It will be another hour or so before we touch down."

"Okay, I'll kill you *then*," he said.

"But then you'll be stuck on an unknown planet,"

Joshua said.

"Everyone else will be down shortly. *After* they wreak havoc on the aliens."

"You haven't thought this through, have you, hero?" Joshua asked. "You'll be down *there* when that happens. I might just drop us off at the nearest population center and let you face down whomever you meet there while waiting for the nukes to drop. And good luck explaining your people's actions if you happen to survive!"

"You won't fare much better."

"So I die sooner," Joshua said. "You'll save me potential torture."

"Take us back to the ship and I'll see that you get a fair trial."

"You can't make that promise, hero."

"It's *Kent!*" he corrected, ripping off his helmet. "*I* was the agent in this ship when you hid in the suit!"

"See, that wasn't so hard, was it?" Joshua asked. "And I'm sorry, Kent, but I'd rather take my chances with uncertain death than with certain death. I've already been sentenced to die *twice* on that ship."

"Maybe I'll just pull the trigger and take my chances flying," Kent said.

"Nope, wrong again, Kent. You wouldn't have

even said that if that was your *real* intention; I'd just be dead now." Joshua said. "Let me help convince you further: That windy noise you're now hearing is us starting our de-orbit burn into the atmosphere. If you take the controls now and try to change the angle of our descent in any way, we'll both be cremated. And might I suggest you find a seat and buckle in."

A sudden burst of turbulence knocked Kent off balance, and he only stood a moment more before holstering his gun and strapping into the copilot's seat. The shaking began in earnest now, and Joshua wrangled the ship into staying the course. Eventually, they broke through the upper atmosphere and suddenly were met with blue skies and clouds, a sight Joshua had never seen before. Kent was looking out each window, taking in as much as he could. Joshua saw Kent's divided attention as an opportunity to put on goggles and an oxygen mask. Then he accelerated into a dive straight toward the trees far below.

Kent woke up with his hands taped behind his back. His feet were also taped together. A side hatch was open and wind was blowing noisily into the pod. The g-force must have caused him to black out when the kid went into a dive. He cursed himself for taking off the helmet. The kid stood over him, gloating.

"Don't worry, I analyzed the atmosphere before I opened the door. I'm going to push you out of the pod now," the kid shouted over the noise. That's when Kent realized he was wearing a backpack on his chest and a chute on his back. "The chute will deploy immediately, and you should try to find water and shelter before night falls."

"What are you doing?" Kent yelled.

"The backpack on your chest is filled with survival gear and food rations, enough for about two months, if you're stingy. Oh, and don't forget to use the water filter if you're thirsty. In the meantime, plant the seeds I've packed and eat just enough of what grows to keep you alive while letting some plants go to seed. This is very important!"

"Let me go!" Kent yelled. "This is crazy!"

"You can try some of the plants and animals on the planet, but I wouldn't suggest it until your body has had a chance to build up its immune system to this planet. I'd give it about a year or two."

Kent looked out the hatch and saw jungle passing far below him.

"It's pretty secluded. Less chance of you running into an intelligent life form," the kid shouted. "You should be at the top of the food chain!"

"Please don't do this!" Kent yelled. "I didn't kill *you!*"

"Much appreciated, Kent! So I'm returning the favor and not killing you. Oh, and before I forget, here's a knife to cut the tape off your hands and feet." The kid put a knife into Kent's hands. Kent tried to throw it angrily back at him, which proved difficult while his hands were taped behind his back. The knife slid harmlessly across the floor.

"I'll hunt you down and kill you, kid!"

"You might want to hold onto this tighter," the kid said as he put the knife back into his hands. He patted Kent condescendingly on the back. "You've only got so much time to cut that tape so you can deploy your chute!

"And by the way, my name's Joshua Hawker, son of Tom and Elise."

Then he put a boot on Kent's chest and pushed him out of the hatch into the open air.

16

Joshua spent the day flying within a five-mile radius, collecting plant samples and observing the wildlife. He noticed that the gravitational pull on the planet's surface was lesser than the artificial gravity on the ship, which had been patterned after Earth's. The planet must have been slightly smaller than Earth, but not so much so as to change the habitability of it. He had been training his leg muscles on the ship for a larger planet, just in case, so he felt even *lighter* than a normal Earth human would.

It took him a few steps to get used to walking, but once he did, he decided to test out how much higher he could jump. He used a distance laser to find a branch fifteen feet tall, and then stood directly underneath it and jumped straight up. He touched the branch at about his elbow. It was pretty exhilarating to feel that strong.

So far, he hadn't seen any signs of civilization, which was a good thing since he was seeking seclusion. He flew low in the valleys and canyons, so he would not be as visible against the sky. In his observations, he had not seen anything that seemed like it could be intelligent life, but he was completely aware of how limited his knowledge of the rules of this planet were. There could be intelligent bacteria, for all he knew.

Before night fell, he wanted to find a clearing in which to land the shuttle, and then analyze his gathered samples until he became tired. Joshua sailed over the jungle, looking for fresh water with a clearing nearby to make a semi-permanent camp.

As his eyes scanned the landscape, the lilting melody of Lacrimosa came unbidden to his mind. He didn't know what brought this on at first, but was suddenly startled to realize he was *seeing* the song written in the landscape. The colors weren't as bright as his drawing, but it was definitely there in the muted colors of nature.

How is this possible? Joshua wondered. It was like he was in the middle of a surreal dream, but he was awake.

Suddenly the trees broke into a clearing and Joshua saw giant earthen mounds shaped into symbols, similar to the earthwork mounds he read about on Earth. He saw a shape that looked like a four with a line bisecting the bottom. He had seen that shape before. He pulled the capsule out of his pocket and located the coin, orienting it to match the mound on the ground. It was a perfect match, and he knew it was meant for him. He found a flat area of ground and landed the shuttle.

Joshua sat and stared at the coin in his hand and wondered what it all meant. How could a civilization separated from Earth by hundreds of light years connect with him in such a strange way?

Then something occurred to Joshua that hadn't before. As he stared at the coin, he remembered the piece of paper folded into a pocket that contained the cryptic binary code on it. The pocket had been just the right size to hold the coin. The coin had been from his father and must have fallen out of its place in the paper pocket. He pulled up the language database on his hard drives, and recalling the time his father had told him of doing research in a nation called Japan on Earth, he looked up Japanese characters first. Immediately, when Joshua pulled up the first page of Kanji, he realized he had been looking at the symbol upside-down: The patterns in their writing indicated so. It didn't take Joshua long to locate the character. It was the symbol for "direction."

What direction? What does that mean? Joshua took a look at the symbol again and studied it. Knowing what he knew of handedness, and ascertaining from the database that Japanese characters were traditionally written top-to-bottom, right-to-left, Joshua deduced how the character would have been written. He knew which line began the character, and which line ended it. *That* was the direction.

In his head existed all of the binary code typed on the paper. It didn't matter that the paper itself had been destroyed. He pulled up the numbers just as easily as he had the digits of pi all those years ago. But now he had a direction in which to read them. He started fourth digit in and drew a line down that curved into the next two columns, then traced a line across the fourth row which angled down sharply, and lastly, back up and across the second row. He recognized the codec as a common audio file, and suddenly heard his dad's voice in his head. "Son," it said.

Joshua repeated the pattern in the direction of the kanji, and as he visualized the code, he heard the message in his head as if it had been played from a speaker.

"I had a dream about you last night. But it seemed like more than a dream… it felt like a vision. I saw you standing between two peoples at war. You were with someone else, standing there boldly, but I could tell you felt very alone. You had a frightened look in your eyes. I wanted to tell you I was there, that you *weren't* alone. I looked around and saw my wife and kids standing behind me. Your mom and siblings. Then I looked beyond them and saw many millions more. But you couldn't see us, couldn't hear us. I knew you had the ability to connect us all, to end the war. I wanted *so badly* to tell you we were *all* there for you. But you wouldn't see anything until you believed.

"Then, the Creator of us all stood before me and told me to conceal this message until the time was right. I woke, troubled at what I'd seen, and wondering how to conceal a message from *you*!

"Haha! This is the best I could come up with, but I'll see if your friend will put it somewhere safe for the voyage. Maybe he could put together a time capsule or something, I don't know. So if and when you are able to get this message, God willing, the time will be right. I don't know what the future holds, but I believe you have an important role to play.

"Joshua, I love you. More than life itself. God be with you."

Joshua raised the shuttle in the air and circled the ship until the "direction" mound was right-side up. The rest of the mounds now made sense. It was a map; directions. Here was a winding river, there a mountain, this mound indicated a distance, this one a change in direction; it was all apparent to Joshua now.

How the aliens knew he could read this, and how

this was all connected to his father's dream still remained a mystery to Joshua. But at least it wasn't a death threat; it felt more like a welcome. This alleviated some of the fears in Joshua's mind, even if it *did* create more questions.

He stored the map in his memory and took off.

17

Joshua followed the landscape markers according to the map until it became dark. He hated to turn on his spotlights, but he didn't want to stop *this* close to his destination. Finally, he saw the rock formation indicated in the earthworks as the destination point. There was a large circle of monoliths with a flat area in the center. This looked like a landing point, just exactly the right size for his shuttle.

Joshua was confused at how this all worked. These must have been built by ancient peoples, judging by the weathering of the stone and the overgrowth on the mounds, but it was obviously a landing pad for a modern shuttle.

He lowered the landing gear and aimed the thrusters down to slow his descent. The jarring of the ship indicated he had touched down. Joshua turned off the engines and unbuckled, but just sat there looking out the windows for a while. The lights only illuminated so much of the jungle beyond the ring of rocks.

He didn't know what to expect when he exited the

pod. Would he be greeted by a group of strange-looking creatures? Maybe even captured? He figured the latter scenario was more unlikely and he decided against arming himself, so as not to look like an aggressor. He took a deep breath and arose from his seat.

Joshua lowered the hydraulic ramp first. One more deep breath, then he turned the handle and opened the hatch. He looked around, and seeing no signs of life, he walked slowly down the ramp and away from the bright lights of the pod interior. When his eyes adjusted to the dark, he saw a figure step out from behind a pillar of rock, and Joshua stopped walking. When he had stopped, the figure took a few more steps into the light.

It was a human.

A female human. Her dark complexion suggested she was indigenous to the hotter clime of the jungle, but her manner of dress was strange for someone tribal, at least according to Earth's standards.

She didn't seem hostile or even remotely dangerous. Joshua ascertained that she might be a representative of the planet's people, sent here to make contact with him. Perhaps she had been expecting to meet with something alien as well, which would account for her coy demeanor.

Whatever the case, Joshua tried to think of how to make contact. Should he offer a hand to shake, or would that be considered hostile on this planet? Perhaps if he smiled, she would know he's not antagonistic? He decided to just stay still and let her be the first to try to communicate.

She took a few more steps forward and looked up at his face. "Hello," she said.

She spoke English?

Elsewhere

Turnabout Volume I

RUSS WOOD

DEDICATION

To Brenda.
You always believed.

IMPORTANT AUTHOR'S NOTE

This book is comprised of two separate but connected stories. You may start with either story and then flip the book over and read the other. Depending on which side you start on, the title is either *Where Else*, or *Elsewhere*. Your experience with the stories might differ from someone who has read it in the opposite order.

So make your choice…

I

Hope was lost.

Marai sat in her New York apartment, angry at everything. Her stupid mom was about to take her on a yearlong trip to live in a jungle miles and miles away from everything civilized. She sent another message to her friend, Ana, across town. This was probably the fiftieth message she'd sent in the past ten minutes, almost as if she was trying to tell her whole life story before she was cut off forever.

It's almost like she wants me to be a hermit!

come on its her job

Her job to ruin my life?

u know what i mean

I do, but why does she have to take me with her? Why can't I just stay here and go to school with you?

i think my dad said u eat too much

*Oh haha. This is so unfair! In a year I will lose my flexibility and get fat and lose my place on the gymnastics team.
I wish I were dead.*

u may get ur wish. did u see the news?

No, what's going on?

turn on ur tube

Marai turned on her set and flipped to the news channel. Amid the stories of wars and turmoil, there were reports of an object in space hurtling toward the planet.

It was about a month away. Some analysts said it would be the closest a meteor or asteroid would ever come to them, others said it was on a collision course.

> *Are you talking about the meteor?*

> *ya. pretty scary huh?*

> *Oh, come on. It will miss like every other one. They always do. I'm doomed to live out a long life of misery.*

"You know service on that thing ends tomorrow, right?" Kit said, as she came into the room holding a box of supplies.

"What's it matter, Katherynne?" Marai said. Her mom hated it when she called her by her name. "We're all going to die in a month anyway!"

"What, the asteroid thing?" Kit said, squinting past Marai at the news report. "It will miss like all the others. They always do. Now put that thing down and help me pack our equipment."

"I'm still bringing this with me," Marai said.

"A lot of good *that* will do you," Kit said, and she bent down to kiss Marai on the head.

Marai pulled away. "What's gotten into you? You used to love to come with me on sabbatical when you were younger!"

"I didn't have a life then," Marai said.

"Oh, I see...Thirteen years old and you're already set for life!"

"Can't you just quit your stupid job?" Marai asked.

"And how would I feed you?"

"Just get a *different* job. Something that lets you stay here!"

"I can't leave my job, you know that. I've spent my entire career at the university studying these people, and I'm not about to..."

"It's always about *you*, isn't it?" Marai said.

Kit sat down and looked into her daughter's eyes. "Are you hearing yourself right now?" Marai looked away. "I'm sorry we have to go off the grid for a year, I truly am. I rely on technology as much as you do. But there's just no communication towers where we're going, and there's no way around that fact."

"I wish Dad were still alive," Marai said. "He'd let me stay home."

Kit looked surprised. "If dad were still alive, he'd be coming with us also. It wouldn't change the fact that you are spending a year away from home. Look, just...try to pretend you're a child again, making new friends and having new adventures. It'll be fun!"

Kit moved the box between them and started pulling things out. "Now help me go through this stuff," she said, and she started busying herself separating items.

Marai stood up wordlessly and walked to her bedroom, making sure to slam her door behind her so her mom would know *just* how angry she was.

She plopped down heavily on her bed and messaged Ana:

I hope it's a direct hit.

II

"Marai? Marai, wake up!"

Her mom pounded on her bedroom door. "The cab is going to be here in thirty minutes! I need you to get up and get ready!"

Marai rolled over and grabbed her phone. She typed:

Are you awake?

She hit send, and the screen read: No service. Her mom hadn't been bluffing, which made it all the more obnoxious when she pounded on Marai's door again.

"Marai, are you even in there?" Kit yelled.

"No, *Katherynne*, I'm gone! And you don't have to break my door down, *sheesh*!"

"I'm considering it if you don't get moving!"

Marai groaned loudly and rolled onto the hard floor. It hurt, but the pain matched her mood, so she didn't care. She pulled on the same clothes she wore the day before, and covered her hair with a big, old, ugly hat rather than do anything nice with it.

It's not as if those savages are going to care what I look like, Marai thought.

Marai opened the door and carried her heavy backpack out into the living room. Her mom was wiping off the kitchen counters.

"The dead rise!" Kit said. "I'm sorry, but we're fresh out of brains." Marai wasn't in the mood for jokes right now, so she ignored her.

"Here's some breakfast. Hurry up and eat it." Her mom handed her a piece of toast with an egg on it, then went back to her hurried cleaning. Marai loved eggs on toast, but showed her mom her displeasure by eating it with slow, labored bites, letting her mouth hang open as often as she could. Manners, shmanners.

"Did you carry our plants over to Mrs. Thile's apartment yet?" Kit asked. Her back was to Marai while she did last minute cleaning, completely ignoring Marai's performance.

Marai closed her eyes. "No," she said.

Kit turned around and saw the apartment was still

decorated with plants. Just then, a knock came to the door. She sighed.

"Well, I guess they'll just have to die," she said. She dried off her hands and answered the door. Marai looked past her mom and saw a cabbie in the doorway. Kit started handing cases to him and then turned back and called for Marai.

Goodbye world. Marai thought. She put on her backpack out in the hallway and followed the cabbie and her mother down to the lobby. A large bus was parked in front of the building.

"Don't tell me we're going all the way there in *this*!" Marai protested.

"No, my cab is parked around the corner, miss," the cabbie answered.

Oh, great, why don't we just walk there? Marai thought.

"He's taking us to the airport," Kit said.

They walked down the busy sidewalk, dodging passers-by while carrying all the equipment. Marai was already tired. Tired of walking, tired of arguing, tired of *thinking!* She cleared her mind and forced herself to just put one foot in front of the other, which didn't require any thought at all. She heard a sound up ahead and looked up. On the corner, Marai saw a street preacher dressed in a robe, shouting to all who passed by.

"The end is nigh!" he cried. "Repent now, while you still can!" Everyone seemed to be ignoring him except for Marai.

"This world will meet its end in flames if we do not change our ways! Wars, pestilence, plagues, famine! Destruction of all you hold dear! Repent ye!"

As they passed the preacher he looked directly at Marai. They continued around the corner and Marai wondered why nobody even looked at the man. He seemed to be sincere, if a little crazy, but did that mean he wasn't human? Marai followed that thought and started to wonder how a person even *got* to that point. She turned around to get one last look at him, and saw he was no longer there.

I guess the end of the world isn't near enough to not take a break sometime.

Marai turned her brain off, turned back around and was startled to see the street preacher standing right in front of her.

"You have a special role to play before the end," he said.

Her mom and the cabbie were still moving ahead, unaware Marai had been stopped by this strange man.

"O-okay," she said.

"You need to find our Savior. Only The Eternal One can save us all." He was speaking in a hushed, intense manner, as if he didn't want anyone else to hear.

"I'll... do that, then," Marai said, breaking his gaze and trying to step past him. He stepped sideways into her intended path.

"I'm not crazy," he said. "I speak only truth."

"Good," Marai said. "Um, I need to catch up to my mom now." Marai stepped the other way around him, and this time he let her pass. She took a few quick steps forward and glanced back to see if he was following her, but he was nowhere to be seen, almost as if he'd vanished into thin air. Were her eyes and ears playing tricks on her?

Maybe I'm the crazy one.

Marai and Kit finally boarded the plane after the hassle of checking in all their luggage and equipment. Marai sat in the window seat so she could watch the city recede out of sight. A few hours into the flight, Marai got bored enough to break her vow of silence with her mom.

"What if they're right?" Marai asked.

"What if who's right?" her mom answered, lifting her sleeping mask and raising her seat up.

"The people on the news. What if the meteor... or comet, or whatever hits the planet and we all die?"

"Sweetheart, I'm *sure* the government has

measures in place to prevent that from happening."

"Like what?" Marai asked.

"I don't know. Maybe satellites with lasers, or space shuttles with rockets, or something. You don't think they would prepare for something like that?"

"I guess so," Marai said. "But how can you be sure?"

"I'm *not* sure," Kit replied. "Honey, why are you getting so worked up about this? It's not as if there's something you can do about it."

"Well, there was that street preacher who seemed pretty sure this was the end of the world."

"What street preacher?" Kit asked.

"The one on the corner."

"Whatever. Sweetie, you can't listen to anything those people say! They've been saying the end of the world has been coming for centuries! And look, we're still here."

"So we just go about our lives, as if nothing could happen?" Marai asked.

"We go about our lives *until* something happens. If everyone shut down the minute something threatened us, the world truly *would* end." Kit leaned her seat back, but didn't cover her eyes. "Now let me get some sleep...I was up early this morning. Unlike *some*one."

"Okay, Kit," Marai said. She leaned her head

against the window and watched the clouds fly past below them.

"That hat is cute on you," Kit said, yawning. "I remember when daddy bought it for you." Marai looked at her mom, who smiled at her and covered her eyes.

Marai leaned her head back against the window and bit her lip so she wouldn't cry.

III

A long flight and bus ride later, Marai and Kit were at the last civilized town they would see in a year. Marai sat on a bench, covering her face with her shirt to keep the dust out of her eyes while her mother arranged for a cab to the next village. There, they would hire a porter to help hike their equipment into the deep jungle to the tribe her mom was studying.

After what seemed like an eternity, Marai's mom returned to the bench and beckoned Marai to a cab parked at the side of the dirt road. The vehicle was very unlike the cab they rode in in New York. It was a rusty, old, cramped car that was so small they needed to strap their gear to the roof. It sputtered and growled like it was barely hanging onto life. Marai crinkled her nose at the smell when they climbed inside.

"Okay, we are in," Kit told the driver in his language. Marai was surprised at how well she still understood the language her mother taught her years ago. The cab driver took off, honking his horn to move the people and animals out of his path.

As soon as they left the town, Marai asked if she could open her window to let in some fresh air. Kit approved, and Marai stuck her head out of the car and took a deep breath. The dense wall of trees around her smelled wet, and she could hear the sounds of rainforest life all around. A flood of familiar emotions filled Marai's heart. For the first time since they left New York, Marai felt... hopeful.

The cab started to wind up a curvy mountain road, and the car suddenly became noisier as it began the steep ascent. Marai pulled her head back in the car and rolled her window back up, leaving it open slightly at the top. Between the noise pollution and the air pollution, Marai preferred the noise, but only *barely*. Her desperate need to escape both caused her to fall asleep.

It was the silence that woke her.

"Are we there?" Marai asked, wiping the drool off her cheek.

"No," her mom answered in English. "Car problems."

The cabbie got out and walked around the car, kicking the rear tire. Kit got out to see what was wrong and Marai followed out of curiosity. The tire was completely flat.

"Do you have a spare?" Kit asked. She used the English word for "spare," since she didn't know the equivalent in his language. There was no such thing as a spare in the village.

"No spare," he answered in English. He looked up and down the narrow road with a furrow in his brow. On one side of the road was a steep dirt wall and on the other side was a forested drop-off.

"Can you guide me down to there?" he asked, pointing to a small section of the road about twenty yards down. The hillside was less steep in that one place, and it was there he pulled off and parked his small car at a dangerous-looking angle. But it was off the road enough to let another car barely pass by, should one come.

"I need you to stay with the car, while I hike back and get help," he told Kit.

"How long will that take?" Kit asked.

"I should be back tonight," he said.

"What will we do until then?" Marai asked, trying out her language for the first time.

He looked impressed. "Drink water, count leaves; just don't leave the road. There are not very nice tribes around here." He reached in his window and pulled out a canteen, strapping it over his shoulder.

"Good luck," he said. "Do not leave the car!"

Marai suspected his concern was more for his livelihood than for their welfare. He tilted his hat forward and disappeared around the corner, walking back the way they had come. After a beat, Kit walked behind the car to look at the deflated tire.

"Marai," she said. "Come here and look at this."

Marai walked to where her mom was and hunched over to see what she was looking at. "Look here," Kit said. She was holding onto what looked like a broken arrow shaft protruding from the inside of the downhill tire. "I don't think the cab driver could see this when it was parked on level ground." She pulled on the shaft and exposed a sharp obsidian tip.

"I think this must have been shot into the tire!" Marai said. "If he had just run it over, it would be stuck in the treads, not the side."

"I think you're right," Kit agreed. "Run down the road and see if you can catch the cabbie so we can show him this. Quickly, before he gets too far!"

Marai stood erect and started running down the road. The wall of trees on the downhill side of the road made it feel like she was running down a strange tunnel. The road continued its curve around the mountainside, and soon the curve exposed something lying in the roadway. Marai wondered at first if this was an animal, but as she got closer, she recognized the figure as the cab driver with an arrow through his neck. His lifeless eyes stared blankly back at her. She covered her mouth so she wouldn't scream out loud, then took off at a sprint back up the hill toward her mother.

Her mom was still alive, leaning against the cab, and when Marai saw her, she started yelling. "Mom, mom! They got him! They *killed* him! He's dead! They killed him, they killed him!" she repeated.

Her mom gathered Marai into her arms, and looked all around the jungle. "Shhh! Quiet, Marai. Quiet down!" Her mom's intense tone was enough to scare Marai into hushing. They both listened, unmoving, to the sounds in the jungle around them. Marai couldn't be sure, but she thought she heard the slow creaking of a bowstring being drawn tight.

"Duck!" Marai shouted. They both fell behind the car just as an arrow whistled over their heads. Her mom reached up and untied the rope holding their gear to the top of the car with one hand. Everything toppled down in front of them.

"Grab your pack and put it on your back," Kit whispered. The glass in an uphill window suddenly shattered and Marai screamed.

Kit helped put on Marai's pack then put on hers.

"We need to create as much distance as we can, as quickly as we can!" Kit whispered. "When I say 'now,' run across the road into the trees and don't turn around!"

"Wh-What about the other stuff?" Marai asked.

"It's just *stuff*," Kit said. She looked into Marai's eyes. "Ready?" Marai nodded. "Now!" Kit yelled.

They felt the arrows lodge in their packs as they ran for safety.

IV

The slope was so steep that their first few steps were about ten feet apart. Marai lost her footing and started to tumble, and quickly lost track of her mother in the thick foliage spinning around her. She bounced off a few trees, which managed to slow her down enough to stand up. She heard her mom crashing through the trees up ahead, and she followed her as quickly as she could. Her steps were quick and hard, and every once in a while she would step on a large leaf and slip backward. She bounced back up and continued running down the hill.

When Marai finally reached the bottom, she saw her mother lying face-down in some ferns. She ran over to her. "Mom? Mommy, are you okay?" she asked.

Her mother stirred and Marai turned her onto her back.

"Ow, ow, ow, careful! I think I broke my ankle!" Marai looked down and saw her mother's foot twisted in an unnatural direction. Marai started to panic.

"It's broken! Oh, mom, it's definitely broken! What are we going to do? They're probably coming after us and we're going to die out in the middle of nowhere, and nobody knows where we are!"

"Angel," Kit said, as calmly as she used to when she put Marai to bed as a child. "We can't panic. We need to keep moving." Marai could see tears welling up in her mother's eyes, but she still managed to sound so calm.

"Help me to my feet and I'll use you to lean on." When Marai had helped her mom up, Kit took off her heavy pack and left it on the jungle floor. She put her arm around Marai's shoulder and looked around and listened.

"There's a river in this valley, up ahead. I think they'll expect us to follow it downstream, back to a village or town. We need to go upstream, but head to the river first."

Marai labored to help her mom to the river. When they got there, Kit said, "Get in the water. They can't track us in the water."

Marai helped her mom into the river, which was about waist deep at the deepest point. Despite the calm look on the surface, it was moving very swiftly underneath. They struggled to fight upstream against the strong current, especially with Kit's broken ankle. Marai had an idea. She pulled off her own backpack and tested it on the water's surface. The foam pad and water-resistant sleeping bag floated.

"Lie down on this and I'll pull you, mom." Her mom didn't hesitate to try, which meant she was probably in more pain than she was letting on. Marai hoped the cold, clear water of the river would help alleviate her mom's pain when she got off her feet. It worked much better, pulling her on her makeshift raft.

Marai wasn't sure if it was just panic playing tricks on her mind, but she kept imagining she heard movement in the trees behind her. She would speed up her wading until she thought she was safe again.

After a while, a loud roaring arose up ahead. The air became wetter all of a sudden, and Marai noticed the water beginning to deepen. She looked over her shoulder and saw a tall waterfall tumbling from what looked like an un-climbable cliff. The pool in which the waterfall fell was encompassed by the cliff, meaning that if they were to continue their progression upstream, they would have to go back downstream and find a way on top of the canyon on land.

Marai hated the idea of making her mother walk again, so she looked around for other options. One heavy tributary of the waterfall fell over a dark outcropping of rock, and Marai swam her mother toward this spot. Marai pushed her head through the curtain of water and saw an opening large enough to hide them both. She came back out.

"I think we should hide in here until we feel safer," Marai told her mom. Her mom nodded and whimpered something, and Marai recognized her mother's behavior of symptoms of early shock. She had to treat her quickly, but hiding was her first priority. She pulled her mom through the water and tied the pack straps to a large root curving from a crack in the rock. She reoriented her mom's body so her legs were resting in a raised position on the pack, and Marai stood on an underwater shelf and hugged her mom's back against her chest, trying to warm her up with her own body heat.

Ten minutes passed. Twenty. Marai felt her mom breaths coming regularly now. Marai didn't know how long she should wait, but fear of being killed kept her in the alcove under the waterfall.

It must have been a few hours later, because the color in the air changed to sunset hues.

Marai's legs shivered from the cold, and she knew her mother's body heat was keeping her alive just as Marai was keeping her mother alive. When Marai wondered for what must have been the hundredth time if it was safe to come out, an answer came. Although it wasn't the comforting answer she hoped for.

Marai could hear muffled voices shouting and soon saw the scattered images of their would-be killers jumping across her lens of falling water. She backed up against the dark alcove wall as far as she could, and clutched her mother tightly.

Her mother stirred and started to speak, "Wha...what's..." Marai covered Kit's mouth, even though she knew the faint sounds were probably swallowed up in the din of the falling water.

Marai watched the figures circle around on the far side of the pond, then one called and beckoned to someone unseen. Marai's heart started to race as a man jumped into the water and started walking toward them. It looked like he had a ghostly white face, but the water blurred out any details. As he came to where the water was chest-deep, Marai began to wish silently her dad were still alive to save her.

Marai's mind raced for some way to defend her and her mom. She could think of nothing. She bent over and whispered in her mom's ear.

"I'm so sorry, mom."

She closed her eyes and waited for death to come. She heard a sharp whistle and waited for the arrow to pierce her. It never came.

Marai opened her eyes and saw the man floating face down, two feet in front of their hiding place, the water turning red around him. His companions were yelling and retreating back toward the canyon entrance. There were a few large splashes in the deepest part of the pond and after a second, some men sprang from the water firing arrows at the retreating men. The attackers ran after them until Marai could see and hear no more.

She waited in silence until night fell and used the cover of darkness to slip her and her mom out from their place of hiding. She swam her mother back to where Marai could touch the bottom and then walked back to where she could pull her mom out onto land.

Next to where Marai climbed out of the river, she saw the body of the man with the white face. The moon cast a pale light on him and she could see now that his face was painted like a grim skull. But there was something odd about his eyes. She crept closer, out of curiosity, and was shocked to see his eyes had been sewn shut. The hair stood up on Marai's neck and she went back to her mother, still lying on the shore on top of her backpack.

"Are we safe?" her mother asked. It was a good sign that she was aware of their perilous circumstances.

"For now," Marai answered, and she set about making a shelter for her mom.

The night was long and sleepless. Marai alternated between brief spells of exhausted sleep and wakeful listening. She kept her body close to her mother's for warmth against the cold night air. More than a few times, she heard faraway sounds in the jungle that caused her to lie awake in fear, afraid to move or even breathe too loudly. She prayed the rudimentary cover of leaves and branches she hastily created was enough to hide them from any hostile eyes.

The thought of eyes brought back visions of the skull-faced hunter, whose eyes were sewn shut. She wondered why a blind man was sent to seek them out in their watery hiding place.

Was he endowed with more powerful hearing, or smell, or something? How was it he was able to walk straight to us? Perhaps it was magic? Do I even believe in magic?

During these periods of wakefulness, Marai replayed the events of the last day over and over in her head. She couldn't seem to shut off the machine that kept feeding her the awful images she had witnessed. It was as if her brain was on "loop." It was only when she consciously forced herself to think random thoughts that she was able to slip into another bout of fitful sleep.

When the first ray of sunlight hit the jungle floor through the canopy of trees, Marai awakened her mom and helped her move into the bright, warm light.

"I need you to help me wrap my ankle," Kit said. The sunlight seemed to revive her spirits as well as her body.

"I think I packed a stretchy shirt," Marai said. She opened her pack and paused to show her mom what had stopped the arrow from penetrating further. Her trusty phone had given its life to save Marai.

"I guess that did you a lot of good, after all," Kit said. Marai couldn't tell if her mom was smiling or wincing in pain, so she put the phone down and set to work. Kit had Marai pull on her foot while she bit down on the shirt from Marai's pack. The fabric muffled her yell, but through the pain, the foot was finally facing the right direction. Kit dropped the shirt from her mouth, breathing heavily and looked down at her foot.

"I guess it was just dislocated," Kit said. "Can you walk on it, then?" Marai asked.

"Oh, no. We're still going to have to splint and

wrap it."

With Kit's instruction, Marai located two small, woody pieces of a palm trunk, which curved perfectly around Kit's ankle. Then they wrapped the shirt around the pieces and tied it snugly. Marai found a forked branch which she broke with her foot into a rough crutch her mother's size. Her mother tried it out and found it would get her mobile again.

"Where do we go now?" Marai asked.

Kit thought a moment before answering. "We need to climb around the canyon and continue upstream. I don't dare take you back through hostile territory. If we can get above the falls, we will be safer. Atl's village is only about fifteen or twenty miles upstream."

Marai recognized the name of the chief of the Tutek people among whom her mom had been working. She knew they would be protected there, and trusted her mom knew where to go.

They crossed to the far side of the river and found a place where the slope wasn't as steep.

They slowly made their way to the top of the canyon, stopping to rest every so often. The air began to be hot and muggy toward midday, and the exertion made their clothes cling to their bodies. Marai was tired and uncomfortable, but she knew she couldn't stop, for her mother's sake. When they reached the top, they headed back toward the river to reorient themselves. The water there pooled into a large lake, and the space created by the water gave them a view they hadn't had underneath the canopy of trees.

The forested mountains to each side of the lake framed a gigantic mountain whose top was shrouded in mist. Marai would have stopped to admire the beauty of the scene in the past, but all she could think of was getting somewhere safe before the mist turned into rain.

Kit led them along the lakeside for a few hours, until it narrowed back into a river. It was tough going, but they pressed forward. There were many areas with undergrowth and fallen trees along the water, which slowed their progress considerably.

Marai had to help her mom over some of the obstacles, and soon she became aware of a growing hunger pushing through the panic.

"Mom, we have to stop and find something to eat," Marai said.

Kit sat on a fallen tree and extended her wounded leg. Marai took off her pack and sat on it, trying to catch her breath. Kit looked around at the trees.

"See that tall tree over there?" Kit asked. Marai nodded. "That grows a skinned fruit kind of like a mango, but they normally are on the ends of the branches."

"I'll climb up and knock some down," Marai said.

"Be careful," Kit warned. "I don't want you to fall."

Marai couldn't see any way up the tall, smooth trunk. The nearest branch was about twenty feet up. She walked around the tree and spotted some of the fruit hanging high above. She attempted to throw some rocks and knock the fruit loose, but they were too high off the ground.

Nearby was a tree with a trunk composed of twisted, connected roots climbing from the ground. Marai found she could climb it easily, wedging her feet between the vines. When she was up high enough, she climbed out onto a branch extending toward the tree with fruit. Where the branch she was on became too thin to support her, she tried to break off another branch to knock the fruit above her loose with, but the branches only bent. She had another idea. She backed up on the branch and stood up, facing the other tree.

"Marai?" her mom called out. "What are you doing?"

Marai answered, "Don't worry, mom."

Marai used to do a balance beam routine in gymnastics where she could run across the beam and launch herself off the end. The wood on the branch was rough enough that she didn't have to worry about her footing, and there was only about six feet she would have to cover in the air. She steeled herself and started to run. The branch she ran on had spring near the end, and she used that to her advantage. She sailed through the air and caught hold of a branch on the other tree. Years of training on the uneven bars gave her the upper body strength she needed to pull herself up easily.

From here, it was a simple matter of picking several pieces of fruit and tossing them to the ground.

The climb down seemed a little harder, but eventually she reached the ground and collected the fruit. Her mother showed her how she had been taught to peel the fruit, and they began eating. It might have resembled a mango in look, but the taste was completely different. This fruit was sour and bitter. Perhaps it was just under ripe. Marai puckered her lips with every bite, but she was too hungry to stop eating.

They drank deeply from the river. Their thirst was

strong enough to toss caution aside.

When they finished, they sat and listened to the rainforest around them. There was no indication on the wind that they had been followed, and so they allowed themselves to relax for a while. Thunder rumbled in the dark clouds above them.

"I think we should make a camp here," Kit suggested. "The village is still a way off from here. It lies at the base of that giant mountain. This big tree should offer enough shelter from the rain, as well as food for tomorrow."

"Could we build a fire tonight?" Marai asked. "I have a waterproof container of matches in my bag."

"If you gather dry materials now," Kit answered. "This jungle's about to become a lot wetter."

Marai set about gathering dry wood and bark, while her mom unpacked Marai's ground cloth, pad and sleeping bag. They started the fire next to the large tree just as the rain started to fall. Fortunately, the tree's thick canopy of leaves protected them from the downpour. Marai noticed the birds of the jungle had stopped singing in the thunderstorm.

The sleeping bag needed to be unzipped and hung next to the fire to dry, and when it was "close enough," they both used it as a cover against the night chill. Marai let her mom sleep on the thin pad so she would be more comfortable.

Despite the fact that they didn't know whether their pursuers had given up looking for them, Marai drifted off peacefully to the tapping sound of raindrops.

VI

Marai woke up suddenly, feeling like she was being watched. She looked all around in the early morning light and gasped when she saw a man, standing in the open, staring at her. He was dressed in tribal garb, and Marai startled, thinking they had finally been caught by their pursuers. Her natural response was to alert her mother, who was still asleep.

"Mom, wake up," Marai said. Not taking her eyes off the man. As she spoke, the man disappeared. Vanished. As if he had never been there at all.

"What is it?" Kit said, sitting up quickly.

"There was a man standing right there, but he disappeared!" Marai said, pointing.

"Which way did he go?" Kit asked.

"He didn't *go* anywhere!" Marai said. "He was there, then he wasn't!"

"Are you sure you weren't dreaming?"

"Unless this is still a dream, no. I was awake as I am now!"

Kit hobbled to her feet with a worried look on her face. "Whatever happened, I think it's time we got moving. Pack up!"

Marai hastily rolled up her sleeping gear and strapped it onto her backpack. She tossed the remaining fruits into her bag. The fire was completely out already, so Marai didn't have to do anything to it. Her mom started moving upstream as soon as Marai got her pack on. Marai was surprised at how quickly her injured mother was moving.

"What did he look like?" Kit asked after they had gained some distance from their campsite.

"He looked tribal... dressed in a loincloth," Marai said. "He was maybe in his twenties."

"What else do you remember?" Kit asked.

"Well, it looked like he had one of those scar tattoos around his eyes."

"What did it look like?"

"Kind of like a...sideways hourglass or something."

Kit was quiet for a while, which was okay by Marai, since it was difficult to run and talk. Her mom slowed their pace, as if in answer to Marai's thought.

"I believe you saw him," Kit said.

"I was just starting to think I made him up!" Marai replied.

"But I don't think we have to worry," Kit said. "He's friendly. He fits the description of a Tutek."

"He didn't seem to be concerned that I saw him. He was just standing out in the open." *Plus, he can magically disappear in an instant if he's seen*, Marai didn't add. *He must be related to that street preacher!*

They continued hiking until they came to a trail groomed into the forest floor. This was a sign they were close to the village. Marai's mom started recognizing landmarks along the trail and pointing them out to her. It had been almost seven years since Marai had been there, so she didn't remember the path as well.

The trail began to widen, and Marai noticed marks carved into the trees off the path. She recognized one and pointed it out to her mom: "Mom, that's the same symbol that was around the man's eyes."

"I thought your description sounded familiar," Kit replied.

Suddenly, the trees opened to a clearing dominated by the view of the giant mountain looming overhead. Marai had to tilt her head back to view the top, and was surprised to find that when she looked back down, they were coming into a large group of huts with a cook fire smoldering in the center. Villagers busied themselves with their daily activities until the nearest one noticed Marai and Kit.

"Kit!" she called out and then repeated over her shoulder, louder. To Marai, it sounded like she was saying "Keet," but she was relieved that the villager at least recognized them. A mob of villagers surrounded them and went through a ritual greeting. Many of the younger children who wouldn't know them stayed back behind their mothers, occasionally working up enough courage to reach out and touch the odd-looking strangers. Marai didn't mind all the attention. She found herself smiling for the first time in what felt like weeks.

Many of the villagers were women, left behind to tend the children and perform domestic duties while the men hunted during the day. Marai remembered not having very much interaction with the adult men of the village in past visits.

"Is Atl out hunting?" Kit asked a woman near her.

"Yes, but the party will be back this evening," she replied. Marai was glad to find she could understand the dialect, despite her years out of practice.

"Is this little Marai?" the woman asked. "She has grown so tall!"

"Yes," Kit said. "Marai, I don't know if you remember Zu, but she was my gracious hostess."

"I remember," Marai said. She might have actually

been saying, "I know," since they were very similar words, but Zu didn't act as if she thought it sounded rude.

Kit explained the events of the last few days to the villagers, and the rest of the day was spent gathering nearby materials to build them a shelter to replace their lost tent. Many of the women kindly put aside their own chores to help out in the effort, and before long, they had an enclosed space to protect them from any weather.

During this work party, Marai noticed that some of the women were topless, which made Marai a little uncomfortable now that she was noticing similar changes in herself. Then she realized she was seeing them through her own cultural lens, and as long as they didn't mind their exposure, Marai wouldn't either.

When, at last, they finished and dispersed to their own duties, Marai had a moment alone with her mother to talk.

"Mom, are we staying here?" Somewhere deep inside, Marai hoped the answer would be no.

"Of course, sweetie," Kit answered. "They built this hut just for us."

"No, I mean...are we just going to stay a few nights and then have someone help us get back home?"

"No."

"But after what happened, I thought you...we

would!"

"Marai, this doesn't change our plans," Kit said. "I still plan on staying out here for a year and observing these people all the same."

"But what about your ankle?"

"They have a medicine man who will help me recover," Kit said.

"You don't have any of your recording equipment!" Marai protested. Surely that would be the deal breaker for her mom.

"In a few weeks when I feel stronger, I'll have a few men accompany me back to the road to get the rest of our gear."

"You're going *back*?" Marai asked, incredulous.

"I thought it was *you* who wanted to go back," Kit joked.

"You know what I mean, mom. Someone tried to *kill* us! I still have the arrow hole in my backpack! You know...the arrow that was meant to kill your only child!"

"Marai, it will be fine. The men of this village are very skilled warriors."

Marai wanted to continue arguing, but just then, Zu came into the hut with food for them. Marai and Kit thanked her and began eating. Marai didn't bother asking what kind of meat she was eating; it was delicious. She devoured her meal ravenously, licking her fingers afterward.

She had plenty of time to find out it was the best dog she would ever eat.

VII

The men came back to the village celebrating a successful hunt. They were happy to see Kit and Marai. Marai was reintroduced to Atl, the chief, and he hugged her warmly. He, like many of the others in the tribe, was only a few inches taller than she, which she knew was pretty short for a man. He had a small, round face, a high-pitched voice, and an easy laugh, and Marai found herself liking him despite her preconceptions of what a chief should be like. He declared that the villagers would have a bonfire in their honor that night, which put the whole village in good spirits.

Soon there was a tall blaze in the center of the village; each villager contributing a portion of their own gathered firewood to the cause. They sang and danced, encouraging a reluctant Marai to stand and join them. She knew she couldn't mimic the dance moves very accurately, but tried her best anyway. Some of the children laughed at her clumsiness.

Marai looked over at her mom, who looked like an entirely different person in the firelight. She was impressed with how good her mom looked when she danced. She would gracefully jump into the air and land hard on her one good foot--the other of which had been tended to by the medicine man--and sway her arms just as the women around her did. Marai was most impressed that her mom did it without a trace of irony. She treated the dance as seriously as the tribe did, and did so on only one foot, nonetheless.

Looking around at the men when it was their turn to dance, she tried to identify the man whom she had seen watching her in the forest. Many of them had scarification tattoos on their bodies, and some on their faces, but none of them had the sideways hourglass around their eyes. Marai looked through them once more and then decided he must have been from a neighboring tribe or something.

After the celebrations, Marai and Kit retired to their hut and went to sleep.

The next day, chief Atl came and spoke with Marai and Kit about their troubled journey. He had heard the details from one of the women in the village, and wanted to make sure they felt safe. Marai had a few questions for Atl.

"When we were hiding under the waterfall, I saw the bad men get chased off by someone else. They even killed the man closest to finding us. Was that people from your tribe who saved us?"

"Yes," he said. "We were told to keep our eyes open for the enemy down near the falls. We do not like them coming any closer to the sacred mountain."

"The man that was killed had a…" she struggled to find the word for "skull." "…*bones* on his face, and his eyes were sewn shut."

"These men are very dangerous. You should not stop running if you ever see one again," Atl said.

"There's more than one?" Marai asked. "Yes, there are many."

"How do they see?"

"This, I cannot explain. Perhaps someone else knows better," Atl said. "These gray hairs on my head do not mean I am wise!"

His infectious laugh caught hold in Marai, and she laughed—maybe a little too hard—at his joke. He patted her on the head and stood up to leave their hut.

"Chief Atl?" She had just one more question. "Is there a man with this symbol," --she drew the hourglass in the dirt--"around his eyes in this village?"

He looked solemn. "You have seen this man?" "Yes," Marai said. "He was watching us sleep."

"You come with me," he said. Kit arose to accompany her daughter. "You stay," he told Kit.

"Mom?" Marai looked back at her for approval.

"It's okay," Kit said. "You will be safe."

The chief led Marai through the village to a small hut hidden behind a cluster of others. He pulled aside the flap and gestured for her to enter. Marai obeyed, and when he closed the flap behind them she was enveloped in darkness. She strained for her eyes to adjust to the dark, but she couldn't make out much of what was in the hut. Her gaze was drawn to a sound coming from the back, near the floor.

"I have brought someone to see you, Xrys" Atl said. It sounded to Marai like his name was "Chris," but with a Z sound at the beginning, in the same way "Atl" sounded similar to "Al." Close enough for her to remember, anyway.

"Who is this?" a voice—Marai assumed Xrys'— spoke from the darkness. His voice sounded smothered, as if he had a swollen tongue, but Marai could still make out what he was saying.

"My name is Marai," she said. "My mother is Kit, the woman who comes to study your people." She held up a hand to protect her eyes from a thin shaft of light shining in them through a crack in the hut wall. *How did he see in here?*

"This is the man you saw in the rainforest," Atl said. "I will leave you alone to speak with him." With that, he passed through the flap and returned it in place.

"Come closer," said Xrys. "My ears do not hear so

well." Marai nervously took a step forward and then hunched down; closer, but not very much.

"You come to me from a great distance," Xrys said, more of a statement than a question.

"New York. It's a big city, far away."

"I know you, child, although you do not know me. I recognize you from before."

"This is not the first time I have come to your village," Marai explained.

"No, from before that," Xrys said. "The first time I saw you, I knew you. You are special. You have a great role to play before the end."

Marai remembered the street preacher. "You are not the first person to tell me this," she said.

"There will be others who recognize you. Some good, some evil."

"I'm sorry, I just... am not sure I believe I am any different than anybody else. And what do you mean by 'role?' What do you think am I supposed to do?"

Xrys shuffled around in the darkness. The movement helped define his shape a little more. Marai was starting to be able to make out the frame of a small body on a floor mat. It didn't seem like he could be the tall warrior she saw in the jungle. He had moved just enough that she could now make out his eyes in a beam of light. There was the tattoo masking his eyes, but his eyelids were closed.

"I must show you, but I need to store up my energy," he said. "Come back here in six days, and I will meet you outside the hut. We will climb the sacred mountain together. Tell your mother we will be gone for two days and a night."

"Do you want me here early in the morning?" Marai asked. She was answered only with the sounds of regular breathing. Xrys must have fallen asleep. Marai quietly bid Xrys farewell and left the way she came.

VIII

Six days in a village without technology felt like three weeks to Marai. She passed the time wandering around and watching the women work then trying to nap through the muggy afternoons in her hut. Her mother told her she could pass time quicker if she got involved in the work of the village, but Marai knew better. Her mom was probably just trying to trick her into being "productive," which basically just meant doing hard work.

The night before she was to depart with Xrys, she had trouble sleeping. She was anxious to learn more about her strange experiences, but a little nervous as well. She didn't know much about Xrys, and she would be spending a night out in the jungle with him. But the fact that she was restless as a result of her trying to sleep through the boredom of the day made any new experience an adventure she looked forward to having.

When the sunlight touched the top of the gigantic mountain, she slipped out from underneath the sleeping bag, trying not to wake her mom. As she tied her sleeping mat to her pack, her mother stirred.

"I wish I could go with you," Kit said.

"I understand, mom; your ankle, and all."

"Please promise me you'll be careful?"

"I promise," Marai said. She bent down and kissed her mother. *How long had it been since she'd done that?* Then she made her way to Xrys' hut.

A tall, muscled man stood with his back to her, looking up at the mountain. He didn't look like he shared the same physical stature as many of the others in the village. Marai wondered if the diminutive Xrys was still inside.

"Are you ready to depart?" The man spoke to her without looking. He had a deep, clear voice. He must have heard her approach.

"I thought I would be going with Xrys."

"I am he," the man spoke, turning for the first time to look at her. He had the same tattoo around his eyes as Xrys had, and he was indeed the man who had been watching her sleep many days ago.

Surely he isn't the same frail man in the dark hut! "There must be some mistake!" Marai said. She started to make her way toward his hut entrance, but he stopped her with his words.

"There is no mistake," he said. "We must leave

now if we want to make our destination before nightfall."

Marai was confused. She looked up into the eyes of this stranger, and saw something in his features that eased her mind. There was a kindness in his expression that she couldn't define, but she still *felt*, nonetheless.

"I promise you will be safe," he said. "This mountain is sacred land. No enemy may set foot on it."

Marai decided she trusted this man—Xrys?— enough to satiate her thirst for adventure, and they set off on a trail leading up the mountain.

Marai was in shape, but she was not used to the higher elevations and warmer climate. The sometimes-steep climb seemed to sap her strength right out of her feet, and she asked Xrys if they could stop and rest after about an hour of climbing.

"That would be fine," he said.

Marai practically fell onto the mountain trail as she sat down to rest. Her canteen water was warm, but it was wet, and so she gulped it down greedily. Xrys still stood on his feet, looking up the mountain trail. He wasn't even breathing hard.

"Is it much farther?"

"Yes," Xrys said.

"I do not know if I can take a day of this," Marai

said. Xrys looked at her.

"Why do you let your body limit you?"

"I suppose my body is not used to this elevation."

"But why are you relying so much on it?"

Marai was puzzled. "What do you mean? My body is all I have to move around with."

"Much of what your body feels, your spirit can overcome."

"I think my spirit is also weak, then," Marai said.

"You *think*. That is the problem. You need to *believe*. Your brain is used to think, your spirit is used to believe. Belief is more than thinking or hoping, it is feeling."

"I do not understand," Marai said.

"When you first saw me in the forest, how did you know I was there?"

Marai remembered back to the morning when she first witnessed this strange man. "I saw you."

"You did not see me until after you awoke and looked for me. How did you know?"

Marai thought back, and recalled the feeling she had when she awoke. "I felt like someone was watching me."

"You *felt*."

The memory came back clearly. Marai had felt his

presence before she saw him. "How does *that* work?" she asked Xrys.

"We are not just made of clay. The Potter puts life into the vessel. Two parts: body and spirit."

"What does that mean?" Marai asked. "How does it apply to me feeling you were there before I saw you?"

"You have a spirit inside your body. It is the energy that makes your body move. It is real, just like the wind is real. Even though you cannot see the air, you know it is there because you can feel it. Your spirit is connected to mine, and to every other person who lives or had lived. That connection let you feel me there."

Marai thought about what he said for a moment. "Did you really disappear?"

"I didn't *go* anywhere," Xrys said. "You just started looking at me with physical eyes, and so you stopped *seeing*." Marai recognized the word "seeing" in the way Xrys used it as being close to the noun "seer." He was speaking in a religious sense, as if in the way a holy man or prophet would behold a vision or revelation.

"Are you a...seer?" Marai hoped she was using the word in the right way.

"I believe *you* are," Xrys said. He looked up at the mountain.

———————————

Marai had a lot to think about during the hike. She had to stop often, and felt guilty that Xrys had to wait for her. At one point, Marai insisted they rest so she could eat some of her rations she had brought along. She offered some jerky to Xrys since he hadn't eaten anything, and was baffled when he refused. *Was he some sort of robot?*

They continued hiking until they were above the tree line, and Marai found herself wading through green, knee-high foliage. Marai could see more of where they were going, and she was relieved to see the top of the mountain just up ahead. They crested the ridge and she saw the giant mountain *still* towering above them. The steepness of the hill had hidden the real mountain from view. Marai was getting frustrated.

"Are we going to the *top* of the sacred mountain?" she asked Xrys, plopping down heavily.

Tears came unbidden to her eyes and she tried wiping them away so Xrys couldn't see she was crying.

"Where we are going from here is on the backside of the mountain. Not much higher, but still far away. Take off your pack," Xrys said. "You can leave it here and retrieve it on the journey down."

"But it has my sleeping gear and food!" she said.

"Physical things you do not need. This is a spiritual journey. They are just a constant reminder that you have a mortal body as long as it rests on your shoulders. Unburden yourself. Trust your inner strength."

Marai was uncertain about leaving her gear on the ridge, but she decided she would have to continue on since she didn't know the way back on her own, and it was apparent Xrys had no intention of turning around. She unstrapped her pack and set it down. She was a little relieved to lose the extra weight, but still worried what she was going to do when night fell.

"Now remove your shoes," Xrys said.

"But I need them to protect my feet!" she protested.

"Your shoes disconnect you from the planet's spirit. You need to borrow from her strength for the last part of the journey. From here on, you walk on sacred ground; ground our forefathers first tread. There is much strength here."

Marai looked at Xrys' unshod feet and supposed the ground must not be too rough if he never wore shoes. She pulled off her shoes and placed them next to her backpack. She then pulled off her socks and draped them over her pack to dry out. She wiggled her toes in their newfound freedom and stood up. The ground was soft and warm.

"Empty your mind," Xrys said. "Do not rely on it;

rely only on your spirit to keep your body moving. No more words, no more thoughts, just feeling."

Marai nodded, and they stepped forward together, unspeaking. After about three miles, she realized she felt no more pain. No longer did her lungs burn or her feet ache. If she concentrated, she could almost imagine she could feel light coming in through her feet and spreading throughout her body. She looked down and couldn't see any visible light, but she sensed it all the same. Everywhere the light touched, she felt strength.

Time seemed to pass in a haze. It felt like they had just begun the journey from the ridge moments ago when Xrys' voice broke through the silence.

"We are here," he said.

IX

Marai and Xrys stood before the mouth of a large cave, large enough to swallow Marai's apartment building whole. A spring trickled out of the cave and fell off the large ledge they stood upon. The sight of such a large cave cut into the side of the sacred mountain put the size of the mountain in a different perspective for Marai. Still, the mountain stretched up above the cave opening for what looked like forever. It was an awesome sight to behold.

"What is this place?" Marai asked.

"This is the beginning," Xrys answered. "It is a good place to start if you are to learn of your place in the Creator's plan."

"The Creator?"

Marai had heard of the ancient beliefs of these people. Just like all the other religious people from back home, they believed in an all-powerful being who was responsible for their existence.

Marai didn't subscribe to any such superstitions, and neither did her mom, even though she had taught

Marai to be respectful of others' beliefs, nonetheless.

"The Creator sees all, he knows the end from the beginning," Xrys said. "He brought us here to this place six thousand years ago."

"You cannot also believe this planet is *only* six thousand years old," Marai said. "Look at the spring that created this cave! That must have taken millions of years to create an opening that large!"

"I have said nothing about the age of the planet." Xrys said. "Come with me."

Xrys led them into the cave. A few bats near the entrance flew out into the open air at the disturbance. Before the cave became too dark to see, Xrys pointed to the walls.

"Here is our history," he said.

As her eyes adjusted, Marai could see many glyphs painted on the smooth walls of the cave. She noticed the same sideways hourglass symbol with stick figures posed on each side. There were other symbols she didn't recognize, but often there were stick people involved in the drawings.

"I thought your people did not have a written language," Marai said.

"You are correct. This is not our record. We tell our stories to our children and they pass them on to their children. They all visit Nuzalem at one point in their lives to learn about our beginnings."

"New…Salem?" Marai asked. "Is that the name of this place?"

"We named it after a place in the old world, much like your 'New York' is named after a place in the old world."

"So you're saying you came here from the old world?"

"We were all brought across the great deep by The Creator," Xrys said. "That is what these pictures say."

Marai looked once again at the drawings on the cave wall. The tallest ones were about twenty feet up. There seemed to be so much information, so many stories, but Marai couldn't make sense of much of it. She doubted Xrys understood much of it either. After centuries of passing stories down orally, much of the original information was bound to be lost and changed anyway. So these were just fables, legends, myths.

"What does any of this have to do with *me*?" Marai asked. He pointed to the opposite wall.

"Here is our future."

She saw what appeared to be hundreds of stick figures divided into two groups. They were armed with weapons of war. In the center of the groups was a dotted circle surrounding two prominent figures. One of the figures had one large eye, and the other had the sideways hourglass etched onto its face.

"This is you," Xrys said, pointing to the one-eyed figure.

"I have *two* eyes," Marai said. She was going to say, "I'm not a Cyclops," but she didn't think he would get the reference.

"This is a seer," he said. He pointed to his eye then to her. "You."

"Why do you think this is me?" she said. "I am *not* a seer. I have never had a vision or revelation. I do not even believe in a 'creator'."

"I know it is you, because it *is*." Xrys said.

She was bound to get nowhere with his circular reasoning. "Then I suppose this other figure is you?" Marai asked, pointing at the one with the hourglass on its face.

"No," Xrys said. "That is the One-Who-Will-Save."

"A savior?"

"Your path is connected to His. You must find Him!"

Marai sighed. "I appreciate you showing me this and having so much faith in me, Xrys, but I am doing just fine without a savior. As much as I would like to be the person you think I am, I am not. I am just a regular person. Marai. That is who I am...not *this* person." She pointed to the drawing. "I am sorry to disappoint you."

Marai walked out of the cave, leaving Xrys behind.

It was too late to journey back to the village, and Marai wondered how she was going to sleep that night. Xrys beckoned her back into the cave after the bats had all departed for their nightly hunt, and explained to her how she could stay warm as she slept.

"You need to use your energy from within to keep your body warm," Xrys said.

"How can I do that?"

"First, you must believe you *can*. Do you believe?"

"I believe it is getting cold and I have no blanket."

"I saw you walk with the light today," Xrys said. "Can you deny it?"

Marai remembered the healing sensation when she walked the last leg of their journey. "I know *something* strange happened."

"All it took was for you to try. And to do that, you had to believe first."

"Okay...fine. I believe I will be warm tonight," Marai said. "Now when do I stop shivering?"

"Lie down on the stone floor," Xrys said.

"The stone? That is even colder!"

"Try your faith."

Marai really wanted to believe whatever he was suggesting she do would work, because she desperately needed to be warm. It was this tiny seedling of wanting to believe that ultimately led to her lying flat on a cold, hard bed. The shivering increased.

"Now what?" she asked. "I still feel cold!"

"Close your eyes. Lay your hands down to your sides. Let go of your body and reconnect to your spirit." Marai obeyed, although this didn't seem to make her any warmer. "Touch your long finger to your thumb, hands palm up, and breathe."

"I *have* to breathe," Marai said, teeth chattering. "I will die otherwise."

"Lengthen your breaths, drink all the warmth of the air in through your nose. Collect it in your lungs, and then release the cold from your body when you breathe out." Marai forced her breaths to lengthen. At first, her breathing was interrupted by stuttering, internal coughs, but she commanded her body to obey until her breathing came regularly.

"Good," Xrys said. "Now take in the light. There is always light in the air--even at night--and you must see it come into your body with your breathing. The light is warmth. You must demand the cold of the stone to become warm to your body."

"How do…?"

"Do not speak. You will undo what is done. Do not *think* the stone is warm, *feel* it."

Marai gave up trying to reason her way through this exercise and instead tried to sense warmth coming from the stone underneath her. To her surprise, the stone began to feel warm, as if it was radiating heat.

"Feel the ground hold you," Xrys said. Marai imagined the stone cradling her, and it almost felt like she was sinking into the solid stone. "Keep breathing," she heard Xrys say. "Breathe…"

Then she heard nothing.

X

Marai stood on the pinnacle of the Sacred
Mountain, overlooking the land. It was an amazing sight.
The sky was clear of clouds and it seemed like she could
see forever in every direction. Being up so high, she could
perceive the curvature of the planet. East and West of her,
she could see the oceans far beyond the jungle. She
wondered which of these "great deeps" Xrys' people had
crossed over to reach this point, and from which island.

As she stood there, she felt a breeze. It seemed she
could almost hear voices in the wind, speaking
encouragement and comfort to her. Then came a voice of
warning. She turned around to see black clouds gathering
in the sky behind her, reaching out like grasping fingers
and choking out the sunlight on the ground beneath. They
moved faster than any clouds she had ever seen, and they
were heading in her direction. She turned to run down the
still sunlit side of the mountain and found she was not
bound by gravity. She didn't even give it a second thought.
She took flight and sailed as fast as she could toward an

opening in the mountain below her.

Behind her, she saw the dark mist gaining on her. Angry cries could be heard coming from the mist. She was so close to safety. She didn't know if she would make it, but she set her face forward and flew as fast as she could. The screaming reached a deafening crescendo.

Marai awoke suddenly, breathing hard. It took her a second to realize where she was, but when cognition came, she relaxed when she realized she had just been dreaming. She looked around. Xrys was nowhere to be seen. She stood and stretched, surprised at how refreshed she felt after spending a night sleeping on rock. She went deeper into the cave to look for Xrys, and when she didn't find him there, she decided to wait until he returned from wherever he was. She immersed her lips in the spring and drank deeply, then went outside and relieved herself behind a shrub, in case Xrys chose this inopportune time to make an appearance. It was frustrating not to have toilet paper, especially since the shrub she had chosen to hide behind had prickly leaves. When she finished she went back into the cave and looked at the drawings while she waited for Xrys to return.

She noticed the drawings were rudimentary, as if the message being told was more important than aesthetics. When she examined them up close, she noticed they were not only stained into the rock wall, but also partially engraved. Someone thought this message was important enough to last for a long time. She tried to make sense of the many stories that covered the walls. There were wars depicted, some groups splitting off, a baby being thrown into lava or something, objects falling from the stars, a man in a garden. She gave up and came back to the drawing that was supposed to be her, according to Xrys.

The eye on the figure was detailed enough to have a visible upper lid, and the shape was accurate enough to resemble an eye, but curiously, it didn't have an iris or pupil. What sort of artist would take the time to chisel eyelids in a drawing of an eye but omit the iris? *It's totally not me*, Marai thought. *I have longer eyelashes. On both eyes!*

Marai looked once again at the figure next to "her." It actually *did* resemble Xrys, with the sideways hourglass on its face. So why did Xrys think it represented someone else? Especially when the figure that supposedly represented her looked nothing like her! She realized she was fooling herself. She knew the icons on the faces were symbolic, but knowing that, she was even more convinced it couldn't be boring, old Marai Gardner.

Marai with only-the-one-friend, Ana, Marai.

Marai the Average.

Marai the Ignored.

Marai the Scared of Spiders. Oh, and of Being Hunted by Blind Shamans.

Marai the Fatherless.

Nothing about her said "unique" or special. She was no more a seer than the poor dog she ate was. If he knew he would end up villager meat, he probably wouldn't have hung around. Her current predicament was proof she didn't have any special foresight. Xrys was sincere, but dead wrong.

Thinking of Xrys, she began to worry. It was nearing midday, judging by the position of the sun in the sky, and he hadn't returned from wherever it was he went. She started to look around for clues of his departure or direction. Looking at the grass around the cave didn't yield any clues as to his whereabouts. She was not a tracker. The ground all looked the same to her.

She went back to the cave and paced for a while. She took a drink from the spring, paced some more, looked at the pictures on the walls again, and then lay down in the grass looking at the clouds. She was hungry. Not to mention scared. She didn't know how long she should wait, or if she should even start back in the direction of the village on her own. She closed her eyes.

Marai didn't believe in any deity, but if one existed, now would be a good time for him/her/it to manifest itself to her. She had always been a proud loner when it came to spirituality, but now she was at a loss of what to do. She came from strong parents who expected her to study out a problem in her mind and then come to her own conclusion, and that was the pattern she had always lived her life by. Normally—if she was being rational—they allowed her to execute her plan of action, and then let her deal with the consequences of that decision on her own.

As scared and alone as she was, she wasn't sure she was ready to start praying to any "Creator" for deliverance yet. Who knew: Maybe the Creator worked a lot like her mom and dad, expecting her to come up with a solution on her own? It was hard to break a lifetime of habit, anyway.

So she sat up, decision made. Marai would find her way back to the village on her own. If Xrys meant to reconnect with her, he could probably find her on the trail.

She started back around the mountain in the general direction they had come, keeping her eyes open for the ridge where she had left her pack and shoes. Because of the elevation she was at, she could see the forested mountains and valleys stretching out in every direction as far as the eye could see. There was no indication of any villages or cities in any of the valleys. It all looked the same to Marai.

Eventually she spotted her pack on a ridge far below her. She trudged her way down to the pack, and as she did so, she started to notice her bare feet becoming sore from chafing against the ground. She hadn't been walking in the meditative way Xrys had taught her. Her mind was too preoccupied with finding her way back.

Marai put her socks and shoes on and then ate all the remaining food left in her pack. She shouldered her pack and looked at the tree line below her. One of the treed valleys led to Atl's village, the others to being hopelessly lost. She really wished she had looked back every once in a while during yesterday's journey, just to see what it looked like from the direction she was now facing. She thought there would be a trail through the brush since they made the journey so recently, but there was nothing she could distinguish. She decided to make an educated guess based on the topography. She looked at the steepness of the valleys, and knowing the valley she came up had a river that moved quickly enough to run clear, she determined she would go down the steepest one. It was her best shot.

When she was inside the trees, a troop of monkeys cursed at her for disturbing their peace.

The familiar sounds of the monkeys and birds was of little comfort to her, but the cover of the trees at least made it feel like she was getting closer to her mom.

The trip through the underbrush was often grueling, only clearing out when the occasional canopy of leaves above prevented sunlight from getting through and feeding the underbrush.

Eventually, she found herself on a trail. It could have been a game trail, but regardless of what made it, it was much easier going than wading through forest growth.

Her feet still hurt, and she could tell it was starting to get late in the day. The last thing Marai wanted to do was try to navigate her way through the jungle in the dark. Besides the nocturnal predators that hunted for scared city girls at night, she had no desire to keep walking for hours in the dark. She hurried her pace.

When the trail in front of her began to be lost in the increasing darkness, and the pain in her legs and back became unbearable, Marai came up with a desperate thought: She needed to do that meditative walk thing Xrys had shown her. She removed her pack and hung it from a tree. Maybe she could find it again, but if not, it was just stuff. She figured that the reason her feet didn't hurt the first day was because they hadn't had as much exposure to the rough ground, so she elected to keep her shoes on her feet.

After about a half a mile, with no discernible

difference in pain, she decided to go the full way and remove her shoes, tucking them into her waistband. She wasn't sure she believed what happened before was because of anything Xrys had taught her or just pure exhaustion and desperation—she had heard of a thing called "runners' high" that runners experienced—but regardless of her doubts, she was willing to try it again. She would believe in it as long as there was a chance she could feel that strange healing sensation again. To do so would require her full commitment to the process.

She cleared her mind and began to walk. Her feet stopped hurting almost immediately. She passed through the trees in whatever direction she felt she needed to go. Marai stopped lending her useless brain to the task of trying to figure out where to go. She was just walking by faith now; hoping her feelings were better navigators than her brain was.

The forest around her became a blur. Time stopped moving in its tedious progression. Even though it was dark all around her, her steps were accurate and sure.

Somewhere along the journey, Marai became aware of a presence just off to her side, hovering outside of her periphery. She would glance quickly in that direction, but see nothing. The presence felt ominous. She imagined she could hear a voice in her head:

You'll never make it. Give up.

Marai tried to pass the thoughts off as her own fears creeping in. Any time she lent credence to the idea that it was something outside of her, her pace slowed and the forest floor started to become painful again. As long as it felt like her own doubts, she could replace them with hope. She pictured her mom, cooking pancakes. She pictured her dad, reading her a bedtime story.

Home.

The feeling of security associated with the thought helped her regain her pace. That was where she was going. Nothing was going to slow her down!

But he's not there. Nothing will ever be the same. What's the use? Stop trying.

She wondered where these nagging thoughts were coming from, and tried again to clear her mind and press forward.

STOP NOW, MARAI!

Marai fell to the ground. The last thought penetrated her soul sharply enough to feel like it was shouted into her ear. She *never* thought of herself in the third person, and she began to be filled with a great dread. She was sure something else was responsible! She could feel it on top of her now, a great, dense blackness pressing her down. She curled up and covered her face.

YOU ARE NOT SPECIAL!

Marai started to wail. As she did so she found it hard to draw air back into her lungs. It was as if the life was being squeezed from her. She was more scared than she had ever been in her life.

I WILL DESTROY YOU, MARAI GARDNER!

Please help me! she pleaded internally.

"Marai?"

Suddenly, Marai could move again. She could breathe. Gone was the presence that held her bound.

"Marai?"

She recognized the voice of her mother calling out to her. "Mom, I'm here!" she yelled.

Marai pushed herself up to her knees and just as she did, her mother fell on her and embraced her tightly. Marai began crying.

"It's okay, Marai! I'm here now! You're safe!"

Kit pulled the hair out of Marai's face and kissed her forehead. Marai became aware of tribe members standing around the two of them. She pulled herself together.

"What's going on?" Marai asked, wiping her tears.

"We came out looking for you when you didn't return."

"I'm so glad you found me!" Marai said.

"At first, when I saw you leaving the village alone, I didn't think anything of it," Kit said. "I figured you had plans to meet Xrys in the forest. But when you didn't come back, I had to come find you."

"Mom, I left with Xrys yesterday morning, right from his hut."

"Yesterday?" Kit asked.

"Marai, *it's been a week!*"

XI

The search party spent the night on a level spot near the place where they found Marai, choosing to let her sleep next to a fire rather than make her travel back to the village. Marai tried to sleep, but questions still nagged at her mind.

Where did Xrys go? Why did he leave me on the mountain? Why didn't mom see him walking next to me?

How is it she thinks I've been gone for a whole week? What was that dark presence I felt?

And the most troubling question: *Will it return?*

The sound of her mother breathing peacefully next to her helped put her mind at ease. As long as she could be with her mom, she was safe. Marai slept through the remainder of the night, but not as well as she had the night before on the stone floor of the cave.

On the trek back, Marai told her mom all about her strange experiences on the sacred mountain. Her mom couldn't seem to believe it had only been one night she spent up there, but neither could Marai reconcile her mother's account that it had been many nights. The only explanation Marai could think up was that perhaps she had been *so* exhausted that she slept through a few nights without knowing it, but it seemed strange that, by her mom's account, it had been five. More likely, her mom was exaggerating how long it had been to guilt Marai, or it just seemed longer to Kit because of her intense worrying.

Regardless, Marai was coming back from this experience with even more questions than she had left with. She was going to have words with that deserter, Xrys!

They came into the camp soon after Marai and Kit had exhausted their conversation. Kit retired to their hut to rest after their journey, but Marai was too upset to lie down just yet. She made her way to Xrys' hut and threw the flap onto the roof, exposing the interior to the harsh sunlight.

She could now see clearly the body of the man in the corner of the hut, lying on the mat.

He was an old man. He looked palsied, judging by his narrow shoulders and his thin arms curled over his chest. He turned his torso toward the sound of her entrance and bade her enter in his strangled voice.

She hurried in and knelt down by him. "Where is Xrys? The tall one, not you. Is he your son? I need to talk to him."

"You do not understand, Marai," he labored to say. "There is no other Xrys."

"Then who is the man who left me on the mountain?" she demanded. She tried to keep the anger out of her voice; this old man wasn't responsible for what had happened to her.

"He is just outside the hut."

Marai thought this joke had gone on long enough, but she had to see what he was talking about. She arose and was surprised to see Xrys standing outside.

"You look now on my inner self," he said.

"What? I do not understand!"

"Come back in the tent with me and look upon my body."

Marai followed him into the tent and looked down at the small body lying on the mat, unconsciously breathing. Marai tried to wake him by shaking his shoulder.

"My body cannot awaken while I choose to be in this state," the tall warrior behind her said. "I am now spirit walking. My body and spirit are separate."

"Then I would not be able to feel you," Marai said. She stood up and attempted to grab his arm as she said the words. Her hands passed through empty space. She tried again. Nothing. Marai stepped back with her mouth open. She thought back through the events of the previous days and realized that she had never made physical contact with him. He was a spirit the whole time!

It was a lot to take in. Years of her philosophies of what life was now had to be reevaluated.

"This is the true me. My *self.* I am still made of matter, it is just finer." Xrys explained. "Usually too fine for most people to even see."

"But *I* see you," Marai said.

"That is why I know you are special," Xrys said. "You can see with your spiritual eyes things that others sacrifice their physical eyes to witness."

Marai thought for a second. "Are you saying those men with the skull faces can see spirits?"

"The soul hunters have their eyes taken from them so that they may see beyond the veil of flesh. They are evil, and they only use their powers to destroy."

"How can I see your spirit?" Marai asked. "I never sewed my eyes closed!"

"Tell me about your father," Xrys said.

Marai didn't expect this question. "He died," she said.

"How?"

Marai didn't want to relive the memory she had been avoiding for five years. "Tell me," Xrys insisted.

Marai sat down on the ground. "I was with him,"

she said. "He took me out to get ice cream. I got the rainbow flavor, and he just got vanilla. I always wondered why he liked vanilla. It was so boring and there were *so* many other choices.

"We were walking down the sidewalk, eating them, when a teen boy approached us. Nothing seemed wrong, but then...then he just...shot my daddy. Pulled out a gun and shot him three times in the chest, for no reason. No reason...just...killed him. Ended my daddy's life right there.

"He ran off. The police never caught him. They told us it was probably a rite of passage to get into a gang or something. Or just a random act of violence."

Marai felt a single hot tear slide down her face. She wasn't even aware tears had been welling up in her eyes.

"What did you do after he ran?" Xrys asked.

"I just...cried. I could not believe he was gone! He was *just* there, eating stupid vanilla ice cream, and then he was gone! How could anybody steal my daddy from me like that? There was nobody else like him! Nobody in the world!"

The tears came in earnest now.

"Do you think the universe could erase such an infinitely unique individual forever?" Xrys asked.

"I didn't *then*," she said. "I did not want to believe it! I looked around for him. His body lay there, but that could not be him. He was just here! Where did *he* go?'"

Marai sniffed and looked up at Xrys.

"I have been looking for him ever since. But I have lost hope, lately. He continues to not be there whenever I look. Why can I see you but not him?"

"He stands on a different plane than I," Xrys said. "I am still connected to the living world. There lies my body, still alive, although crippled and aged. But I believe if you hone your gift, you will see him someday."

"How do I hone my gift?" Marai asked.

"It is just like a muscle. If you exercise it, it will become stronger. You may even learn to spirit walk as I," Xrys said. "But before that, you need to learn more about what is real. It is why I took you up the sacred mountain."

"Yes, I had plenty of time to look at the cave paintings after you left me!" Marai said. "Why did you leave me up there alone?"

"You had to learn to walk by faith, on your own," Xrys said. "There comes a time in every child's life when they must let go of their parents' hands and take their own steps. No growth can come without exercising your own faith."

"My mom said I was gone for a week!" Marai said.

"You slept long to collect spiritual strength for the battle that lies ahead."

"You mean, the...dark presence? You *knew* I would be attacked and you *left* me?"

"Everyone called to this work has a wrestle with the Destroyer. I did not know it would happen then, but I imagine the Destroyer particularly wants you dead. Or worse, unbelieving."

"Okay, I am ready." Marai said, standing up and looking him in the eye. "Tell me what is 'real' so I can understand just what is going on!"

"Meet me here in a week," Xrys said. "I need to collect my strength."

"I was afraid you were going to say that," Marai said.

XII

Marai busied herself weaving a new sleeping mat that day. Zu taught her how to locate the right kinds of fronds and how to fray and weave them tightly, so that they created a soft surface for her to lie on. It took most of the day, and when her mom passed by she stopped to admire Marai's handiwork.

"It looks good," Kit said. "You should have it ready in time for bed!"

"Thanks, mom," Marai said.

"You should wrap up what you're doing in a bit, because it's time for dinner."

"Already?" Marai asked. Time had flown by.

Her mom just raised her eyebrows and walked off with a smirk on her face. Marai hated it when her mom was right, but she still smiled, despite herself. She finished the row she was on and went to eat.

That night she had a completed mat to sleep on, and the next morning she had a mission; to stay busy for a few more days.

Marai started shadowing some of the girls around her age in the village, learning to perform some of their daily chores. They spent the mornings gathering dry wood for the evening cook fires, and then gathered different plants that grew nearby for eating. They showed her how to distinguish the edible ones from the poisonous ones. There was one leafy stalk that they would break off and chew on while they gathered the rest. It was really sour, but Marai kind of liked it. It made her salivary glands work overtime, and she would suck down the excess fluid, now flavored.

She had grown particularly fond of a girl named Chetl. Chetl was about her age, and regarded Marai as somewhat of a novelty. She would laugh at Marai's accent sometimes and tease her when she did things incorrectly.

When the chores were finished, the kids would take her down to the river to play. There was a tree that hung over the river in one deep spot, from which they ran off and splashed down into the water.

They would gather clay along the banks and make pots by coiling ropes of clay around and around and then connecting them by smearing the walls with sticks. At first, Marai thought this was just for fun, but then she saw that they would bring their finished earthenware back to the village to dry next to the kiln before being fired. Even their play had a practical purpose.

Marai learned how to make a rude net, with which she could catch fish for mealtimes. She enjoyed the taste of the fish from the river, much more than monkey or—shudder—dog meat. The only wild game she didn't have an aversion to eating was boar. To her, it tasted just like pork products found in her local supermarket.

While many of the fruits, roots, and leaves they harvested were unfamiliar to Marai, they were not entirely unpleasant to eat. She ate them first out of obligation, but soon found that the flavors were quite good. Her palate was not used to these unique flavors, but she enjoyed them, nonetheless.

Near the village grew a large patch of wild strawberries. At last, Marai could appreciate something she was familiar with, and since they grew in such abundance, she indulged herself. They were plump, fresh, and juicy; much better than the imported ones from home that grew moldy after two days.

Marai learned how to make various useful tools using things found in the jungle: Woven straps of bark became a backpack, braided bark became a way to climb a branchless tree, a dry stick and a makeshift bow became a way to make a fire without matches. Chetl showed her how to recognize small-game trails and set snares. While they were checking their snares one day, Chetl asked Marai an interesting question:

"What is the outside world like?"

Marai didn't realize how foreign her life must be to someone who lived her whole life in Chetl's circumstances, although at times she *had* wondered what it would be like to travel back in time and show someone a piece of modern technology, like her phone. It occurred to her that this was a very similar situation to her hypothetical one, but now she was without anything to show Chetl in order to demonstrate just how amazing technology was. So she just tried her best to describe it with a very limited vocabulary.

"We have these things you can hold in your hand that let you talk to other people across the world. They show…"—she couldn't find a word for pictures or video—"You can see people moving really small on them and they have anything you want to know on them. Anything in the whole world!"

It was the best description she could give for the most advanced technology she knew of.

She thought it was sufficient to impress Chetl.

"Do people live together in tribes?" Chetl asked.

Marai was slightly disappointed that Chetl didn't seem interested in mobile devices. *If only mine hadn't been destroyed by an arrow!* Marai cursed inwardly. But she resigned herself to answering Chetl's simple question.

"We don't really separate into tribes. We all just kind of…live together."

"Do you all love each other?"

The question caught Marai off-guard. She wanted to tell Chetl how amazing her world was, but in that regard, hers was a far inferior culture. Marai only knew a few of her neighbors in her apartment building, and she couldn't rightly say she *loved* any of them. The closest she came to loving someone outside of her family was her friend Ana, and Mrs. Thile, who used to watch her when she was younger. Nothing like the relationships Chetl shared with her entire tribe.

"No," Marai replied honestly. But then she proceeded to tell Chetl about how easy it was to get any type of food she wanted in the city, how the temperature of her home was always just right, how large the "huts" were, how easy it was to travel, and how you could trade with someone to do just about anything you wanted, including doing your hair for you.

"Other people do your *hair* for you?" Chetl asked.

Finally, Marai had found something from her world Chetl was interested in. Marai told her all about beauty salons and hairstyles for the remainder of the day.

———————

Before she knew it, a week had passed. Xrys met her outside of his hut and beckoned for her to walk with him.

"I had better not go very far," Marai said, recalling their last excursion.

"We will not go very far, just to the river."

Marai didn't wait to get there before she started asking the questions that were on her mind.

"Tell me about this 'Destroyer,'" Marai said. She knew from experience that this was a very real presence, and not just something she conjured up in her imagination. It scared her.

"There are two unseen forces at work in the universe; the Creator, and the Destroyer. The Creator made all that is, including us, His children. The Destroyer only works to angrily break down what is built, and he concentrates his wrath especially on us. Most people do not know the true identity of these beings, but all serve one or the other, knowingly or unknowingly. When you live your life to build up others and make a better tomorrow, you serve the Creator. Those who tear down, who kill, who profit from others' loss serve the Destroyer."

"Through many generations, we have passed down our knowledge of the Creator and the Destroyer, so that our children would not come to think of our beliefs as superstition."

Marai blushed when he said this. Just now she was starting to understand there were many things she didn't know, and was feeling humbled at her previous arrogant stance on religious beliefs.

"It is important to make a choice when you come to this knowledge. Those who have a sure knowledge of The Creator and choose to serve Him can be His greatest assets. Those who knowingly serve The Destroyer, however, can be very dangerous. They are given artificial powers similar to spirit gifts, but they must often pay a dark price."

"Like sewing their eyes shut." Marai said.

"Among other things, yes. They want to see what comes naturally to you."

"I do not see people with my eyes closed," she said.

"You *could*. Maybe you don't know what you are looking for. Perhaps you have never thought to try. It rarely occurs to most people to attempt to do things beyond their physical abilities. Sadly, many spirit gifts go unused because of ignorance or unbelief."

They came to the river and Xrys stopped walking. He gestured to the river.

"This is where the tribe found me, many years ago. I was not originally of the Tutek tribe. When I was born, I was born into the Lamek tribe, or those whom you know as the enemy. I was crippled and blind, and normally they just abandon all who are born in such a way to the wild beasts, but they had been told by the Destroyer of my path, and sought to disrupt the Creator's plan defiantly. After my birth, the Lamek tribe determined to take me up to the Sacred Mountain to spill my blood in the place of beginning, in order to desecrate the ground so that they could finally make passage onto the Sacred Mountain."

"They were intercepted by the night guard. A cry went out and a battle commenced which took many, many people from the Tutek people. They used to number in the tens of thousands, but now they are down to the one village you know. They who lived fought valiantly and thwarted the plans of the Lamek. Ultimately, those who served the Destroyer were forced to abandon their plan and they tossed my helpless body into the river to drown as they retreated. A girl who would later become my adopted sister witnessed this action from her hiding place among the trees, and she plucked me from the depths and breathed life into me."

He continued: "When she brought me before the chief, the plan of the Lamek then became known. I was adopted by the Tutek tribe and raised as one of their own. I was taught the ways of the Creator, and this true knowledge, combined with my physical weaknesses, made me aware of my spirit strengths. Being unable to use my physical eyes, I learned to perceive spirit matter with my spiritual eyes. Being unable to use my physical legs, I learned to walk in spirit."

"And you think I can do the same?" Marai asked.

"I have seen you do great things; things no able-bodied person should be able to do. I watched from a distance as you took flight from the mountaintop to escape the Destroyer," Xrys said.

"Wait...how did you know about my dream?"

"You were not dreaming. You left your body and went on a spirit walk."

Marai remembered how vivid the dream seemed. She couldn't recall ever having a dream before where she could feel wind blow. Then another thing struck her: "I could fly!" Marai said.

"The forces of this planet do not have as strong a hold on our spirits," Xrys said. "You can travel faster because you are lighter." To demonstrate this, Xrys lifted from the ground and floated over the river to the other side.

"That is amazing!" Marai exclaimed. "Why have

you not shown me this before?"

"First, you needed to believe."

"How did I do this?" Marai asked. "Do I have to be up in the cave?"

"It takes much strength," Xrys said. "You need to be physically strong to leave your body for a period of time. The cave gave you strength and held you safe as you went on your journey. But the longer your body and spirit stay separate, the weaker your body becomes. You must sacrifice physical strength to gain spiritual strength."

"How far can you travel?" Marai asked, remembering how fast she had been flying. "Could I travel to New York?"

"The further you travel, the weaker your body becomes. They are not meant to be too long or far apart. It would take a great sacrifice to travel that far."

"Teach me," Marai said.

Xrys floated back over to her. "Lie down," he said. Marai prostrated herself on a soft spot on the forest floor and closed her eyes.

"Do I need to fall asleep?"

"It is similar, but more meditative. You cannot abandon yourself completely to slumber. You must keep a connection with your mind without relying too much on it."

"How?"

"Very similar to the first time. You must abandon your words and thoughts. Use only images and feelings. You saw me across the river a moment ago. Imagine yourself standing there, the ground under your feet, the sky above your head. Use your surroundings as reminders of the world around you. Listen to the flowing of the river, feel the breeze on your face. Now let go. Release yourself from your physical self. Believe."

Marai started to feel like she was rising off the ground. She felt like she was whirling and turning in empty space, unfettered by gravity. She had felt this sensation many times before in her own bed back home—right before she fell asleep—but now she didn't dare open her eyes in case it was real.

She imagined standing on the bank of the river, tried to imagine what it looked like in her mind, and while she was conjuring up this image, she became aware of a blur of light glowing through her eyelids. She tried to focus on the image, tried to squeeze her eyelids tighter as if to squint, but she still couldn't see what was before her. Her eyes didn't instantly react the way they always had before. It was painfully frustrating. How had she done it before, if she even had?

She was about to open her eyes and tell Xrys she

gave up, when she remembered what he said about letting go of her words and thoughts. This had to be as natural as a dream, conjured up in the mind's eye. She also remembered that she wasn't supposed to have eyes or eyelids, not in the same way she always had. She looked once again at the image and stopped trying.

Suddenly an image of the jungle broke into her vision. There stood Xrys next to the river, although he seemed to be glowing now, and near his feet, she saw herself lying on the ground, breathing peacefully. It was the scene she had hoped to see, but didn't really expect to.

She looked around in awe and then noticed they were not alone.

XIII

"This is what is real," Xrys said. "Do not be alarmed."

He must have noticed the panic on Marai's face when she saw hundreds of warriors walking through the trees. They all glowed—similar to Xrys—except with a different color. If what she was "seeing" was, indeed, color. *If* she was even "seeing."

Some had stopped to look at Marai standing across the river. A few smiled at her. She relaxed a little when she realized they meant her no harm.

"These are the spirits of those who have passed on," Xrys said.

"Have they always been here?" she asked. "I thought spirits went to someplace in the sky."

"Spirits walk among us at all times," Xrys said. "This is their home. Many are as unaware of the living as we are of them."

"You mean… they cannot see us?"

"No. They exist in the physical world, but their eyes cannot perceive the living. Some may at times, like you can."

"How could *you* see me?" she asked. She was completely confused by the laws that governed the universe.

"It is like I mentioned before; I still have a link to the living world because of my body. I stand at the midway point between life and death, as you do now."

Marai looked down at her prostrate body, then realized she had somehow traveled back across the river without stepping foot in it, or even realizing she had moved. It was an odd feeling, looking upon herself. She held up a hand and looked at her spirit "body," realizing she was wearing the same clothes, except brighter.

Your spirit projects the image you expect to be. The way you see yourself. She heard Xrys' voice in her head, responding to her silent question.

Can you read my thoughts? Marai thought.

There is no need for speaking here. Voices are a physical thing.

"I am not sure I am comfortable with you in my head," she said aloud.

"I will continue to speak like this, if you wish,"

Xrys said. "But I should add that you can block others from reading your thoughts if you just desire it."

Marai desired it. She wasn't sure she was ready to let Xrys know she thought he was attractive just yet. Xrys laughed aloud.

"Maybe your desire needs to be stronger," Xrys said. He laughed even harder when she blushed. "There you go! I am *completely* shut out now!"

"You should have warned me," she said sullenly.

"I am sorry," he said.

She changed the subject: "How do we know if these are good or evil spirits?"

Xrys looked around at the warriors and beckoned to one. "Marai, I would like you to meet Tutek. This is the great chief of the Tutek people."

A stately-looking spirit suddenly appeared in front of her.

"It is a pleasure to meet you, after all these years of waiting," Tutek said.

Marai didn't know what to say. It was all still very strange to her. She offered her hand, and was surprised when she felt his hand grasp hers. *Spirit matter can feel other spirits.* She thought of something to say.

"Did you write those prophecies on the cave walls?" Marai asked Tutek.

"No. Those were written long before we settled here. It was my decision to make a spiritual journey back to the beginning when I feared my people's faith in the Creator was waning. I am afraid much has been lost, but we have made our home here ever since, many years ago."

"This is near where the battle for my life was fought," Xrys said. "The ground has been sanctified by the blood of many Tutek people who sacrificed their lives to protect the Creator's plan. No evil spirits feel welcome here, so they do not linger. A spirit only feels comfortable in a place where his or her master is being served."

Marai looked again at the people wandering the forest. Beyond the original hundreds she first saw, she saw—or rather felt—the presence of many thousands more. This must be how the skull-faced man sensed her. "What do they want?" she asked.

"They wait for the time when they can be redeemed. When the Destroyer will be bound and mankind will know peace forever. Most of all, they wait to live again."

"Live again? As in… be alive?" Marai was enjoying the pain-free freedom her spirit body now had, and could not imagine what the benefits of reentering her body could be.

"It may seem liberating to be in this state," Tutek

said, "but after three thousand years of not being able to smell the wet leaves, to taste food, to share the warmth of a bed, to create and raise children, I can attest that this is not the Creator's final plan for His children. Why would He create for us physical bodies if we were not meant to keep them?"

Marai could see his reasoning. She had been unaware of the cons of losing one's body, and just the idea of not eating her mom's breakfasts again seemed like a bleak existence, indeed.

Yet, despite all of these incredible revelations, Marai still didn't see how she fit into the big picture.

"Why me?" she said. "What does any of this have to do with *me*? How do you know that is a drawing of me on the cave wall? How do you know it is not a depiction of some person and event that happened long ago?"

Xrys hung his head. "We do not know," he said. "We *believe*."

"Are there *any* spirits here with answers? Like someone who drew the pictures?"

"We do not know where or who they are," Xrys said. "Marai, the reason I...*we* believe it is you on the cave wall is mostly a work of faith, I admit. The Creator has never revealed Himself to us and spoken his word. We believe he expects us to work it out on our own, and then he will help us. But this belief is not without merit! Many of the things depicted on the wall we have witnessed happening, including...including my sacrifice in the river." Xrys looked her in the eyes with an earnest expression on his face.

"The end is coming, Marai. We are nearing the end of the drawings. The Destroyer is fighting with the rage of one who is near his end! My tribe is the last of the Tutek people, and we need you to guide us! If you are not the one sent to meet He-Who-Saves, then we are all lost. Please, please be the one!"

Xrys fell at her feet and sobbed.

"Please!"

XIV

Marai walked with Xrys back to the village in physical form. She was exhausted and hungry. The few minutes she had spent spirit walking by the river equated to a few hours in the real world.

"The object falling from the stars," Marai asked Xrys. "Is that how we meet our end?"

"I believe it is the beginning of the end, yes," he answered. "Followed by a rendezvous at the Calendar."

Marai looked at Xrys differently after seeing him weep in the jungle. No longer was he the self-assured man who had all the answers, but instead was a frightened boy doing the best with the information he had. His faith was inspirational. Although he had lived his life aware of the spiritual realm, he still had many questions of his own. Seeing he was on a journey for answers made her more willing to work alongside him.

"What is the Calendar?" she asked. She hoped she wasn't misunderstanding the word.

"It is a structure two days downriver, through

Lamek territory," he said. "You must travel there when you see the heavenly sign."

"Marai, there you are!" Kit said, approaching her. She hadn't seen Xrys walking next to her, and when Marai looked, she noticed he was gone to her, too.

"What's up, mom?" she asked.

"I just was going to ask you if you could help me husk these fruits for supper," Kit said. She looked up from the fruits she was holding. "Marai, are you okay? You look sick."

"I'm okay, mom. Just a little tired is all," she said.

"Well, I'm glad you're okay, because my ankle has healed up and I was planning on going back to see if I could salvage some of my equipment tomorrow, and I don't want to be worrying about you the whole time I'm gone."

"You're *really* going back? Mom, it's probably all gone by now!"

"I still have to look," Kit said. "Don't worry about me, Marai. Atl is sending his best men with me! I'll be fine!"

That night, Marai asked her mom to braid her hair. It was nice to feel the familiar tugs on her head which she used to complain about when she was younger. She had taken her mother's love for granted growing up, not acknowledging all of the little things she did for her.

When Marai was really young, her mother stayed at home with her, and would always have a smile and a snack for Marai when she came home from school. To Kit, being there for Marai was more important than pursuing her own career. She still did research for the university on the weekends and taught the occasional night classes, but that was only part-time, and during times when Marai's dad was home to watch her.

After Marai's father died, Kit had to start working full time in order to provide enough to raise Marai. She would come home exhausted from work, but somehow, still find the energy to help Marai with homework and make dinner. Occasionally, her mom would play card games with her or take her out to the park to play. Marai used to resent that they couldn't afford to do more exciting things, but now she realized her mom had done all that was in her power to provide Marai with a happy home life. Marai felt guilty for not realizing how everything her mother did was just for her, including taking a yearlong trip to the rainforest.

While her mom continued to work on her hair, Marai simply said, "I love you, mommy."

Marai watched her mother leave with an entourage of thirty guards the next day. She still worried about her mother, so before she was out of sight, Marai called out to her mom to be careful. Her mom waved at her and smiled.

Marai wasn't sure how long her mother would be gone, so she decided she would fill her days with activity, as she had before. Marai walked to Xrys' hut and found him asleep—either gathering strength or spirit walking—so she decided to leave him alone and spend the rest of the day with the children of the village.

Marai met her new friend Chetl over by her hut and asked her if she wanted to do something fun. Chetl seemed really interested in Marai's braid, so Marai braided Chetl's hair like hers. Chetl admired her new hairdo in the calm reflection of a pool.

Chetl and Marai set a few snares along trails near the river, which they would check the next day. They wandered the jungle until Chetl heard the cry of a Puma on the hunt, after which she hurried them back to the safety of the village.

That night, after Marai had eaten dinner, she went to her hut and lay down. The busy activity of the day had made her tired. Sleep came easy.

Marai woke when she felt someone watching her. It was still very dark outside, but she was instantly alert when she sat up. Xrys stood at her doorway with a concerned look.

"Marai, you must leave the village now!" he said. "The forces of the Destroyer come this way!"

"What about my mom?" she asked. She was already up and shoving things into her new woven pack, even though she didn't want to be.

Xrys said, "I was watching her depart to make sure she was safe, and when her party was over the bridge, I felt darkness behind me. I saw soul hunters drop from the trees and signal to many others to come out of hiding. Then they turned to me. I escaped them and flew here as quickly as I could, but even though they are constrained to running, they should almost be upon us!"

"What about the others!"

"You must leave *now!* It is *you* the Destroyer wants dead! They *cannot* find you here! I will sound an alarm when you are clear of the village."

Marai picked up her pack and ran as quietly as she could toward the Sacred Mountain. Xrys ran alongside her, and when she was far enough away from the village, he turned to her.

"Marai, I must leave now," Xrys said. Deep down, Marai felt he meant something deeper than just leaving her side. "Walk by faith and the Creator will guide you. Look to the heavens."

Xrys disappeared from in front of her, and seconds later, she heard a strangled voice shouting with all the strength a small, broken body could muster. The cry continued for a few seconds then was cut off abruptly. Shouting and screaming began to echo up the canyon.

Marai buried her face in her hands and wept bitterly for a man who would never taste food again, whom she would never walk with in the flesh again.

At least he was free from physical pain.

XV

She had to know the fate of the others, so she climbed a tall tree and sat in a cradle of branches. Then she closed her eyes, slowed her breathing and emptied her mind. It was really hard to ignore the thoughts in her head, but she forced herself to meditate.

Before her visage, light appeared then came into focus. She stood on the forest floor below the tree. She glanced up to make sure her body was safe, and when she saw it was, she ran back to an overlook near the village. When she came near, she saw flames engulfing some of the huts. Some screaming and cries for help still pierced the air above the noise of the flames. Her eyes were drawn to movement below her. She was relieved to see Xrys leading others to safety.

Then she noticed something else. The color he glowed was different. It matched the others' she had seen in the forest who had passed away. Those who he led also glowed the same.

Xrys' manner was not hurried or panicked. He

walked slowly, leading an individual from the village with his arm around their shoulders in a comforting manner. He would lead them to where others had gathered, away from the death and carnage, then return and bring another. She saw Xrys bring Zu, then later Atl. Atl must have bravely stood and fought for as long as he could. He was not wearing his easy smile.

Marai's heart sank when she saw Xrys come from the village holding the hand of Chetl. She noticed Chetl still wore the braid in her hair that Marai had braided earlier that day.

All of the villagers stood now with Xrys, watching their homes burn to the ground. The Lamek warriors still ran through the village, looking for any survivors to kill. They started to extend their search beyond the borders of the village, and Marai was relieved to see the soul hunters could not perceive the spirits who had passed on. They crept past them and left them standing where they had gathered.

They must only be able to see the souls of the living, she realized. Just as she was thinking this, she remembered her own state of being, and watched in shock as a soul hunter below her raised his gruesome face and burned his fearsome gaze into her with his sightless eyes. He yelled to his companions, but Marai knew they could not set foot on the Sacred Mountain. She bravely stayed where she was as they all ran up and halted where the mountain began its incline. The first soul hunter removed something from a bag around his neck that looked like a human heart in the firelight.

"Marai, you must run now!" Xrys shouted to her. "They are about to desecrate the ground with my blood!"

The soul hunter spoke in a guttural voice and then plunged a dagger into the heart he held, dripping blood onto the mountainside. Marai knew this was her cue to run.

Marai began to run up the hill back toward her body in the tree. She heard footsteps close behind her, and remembered she was not held to the physics of mortality. Her steps became longer, and soon she was sailing over the forest floor, with nary a footstep required. She looked behind her and saw the distance between her and the murderous horde lengthening, and knew this would buy her a few more moments to craft a plan.

She realized almost immediately that if she were to reenter her body when she reached it, they would have her cornered in the tree and kill her. There was always a chance that the only people who could see her now in the dark were the soul hunters, and those following them would continue to follow them despite the fact that they couldn't personally see anybody running ahead of them in the dark. She had to hope the thrill of pursuit would lead them past her body without them noticing it in the cradle of the tree. She would then have to find a way to double back to reclaim her body after they had passed by it.

With this plan in place, she made sure her pace was slow enough for them to keep her in sight, but far enough to be safe. The limitations of their mortal bodies kept them from matching her speed, so she slowed down to their speed when she felt she was at a safe, yet visible distance.

She realized as she flew, that the closer she came to her body, the more strength she felt. She knew how to easily locate her body just by the connection her spirit had with it. They truly were meant to be together, operating as a whole. Because of this knowledge, Marai led her pursuers in a direction angling away from her body, lest they see or hear it. When she saw they had safely passed by her mortal hiding place, she corrected her course to the top of the Sacred Mountain.

She was amazed by the stamina of her pursuers. What had taken her most of a day in the flesh, they covered in hours. She passed the ridge where she had left her pack that day, but instead of turning toward the cave, she continued straight to the peak. There were no clouds that night, so the pinnacle was clear above her. It pointed to the stars and slivered moon like a gigantic arrowhead.

The further she got from her body, the weaker she felt. It wasn't like physical exhaustion, but rather a slowing of her speed, a clouding of her thoughts. She forced herself to concentrate on her destination and set her gaze on the peak. At last, she reached the top. She looked around at the night sky. It felt like she was being thrust out into space by the planet like an offering to the heavens. The stars flowed around her in a twinkling band.

The beauty of it all almost made her forget her situation. She looked down the mountainside and saw the servants of the Destroyer ascending toward her like familiar, black fingers. They soon came close enough that she could hear their shouts and make out some of the painted faces of the soul hunters leading the mob. She scrambled to think of her next move, but her mind couldn't focus. She kept trying to think of something, *any*thing, but nothing came.

Where's Xrys when I need him? she thought.

Now *you let me in?* came a response in a familiar voice. Marai was overcome with relief.

Xrys! Please...help me think of something!

What did I tell you about thinking?

The horde was near enough they started nocking

arrows. Marai saw the tips of the arrows glowing, and she imagined they had a special power meant just for spirit matter.

I should not think, I should feel. Xrys, now is not the time for riddles, tell me what to do! Marai thought. The closest few pulled back their bowstrings.

I do not know. This is your trial, Xrys answered.

I need to...

They aimed at her.

...need to...

One soul hunter smiled grimly.

...trust The Creator.

"You are not welcome here!" she shouted. "This is holy ground!"

Marai stretched out her arms, closed her eyes, and let her head fall back. She felt comfort enter her heart, and she opened her eyes and looked toward the heavens.

Suddenly, directly above her in the night sky, a light blazed brightly. Everything around her was illuminated and the soul hunters dropped their bows in horror.

Marai, seeing they were overcome with confusion and panic, took a leap of faith in the direction of her body.

XVI

Marai sailed over the confused warriors who were too scared of the bright light in the sky to notice her anymore. Some of them started to panic and run down the mountainside, and Marai quickly flew past them, heading toward her body. Her speed increased as she got nearer to the tree line and her body. The Lamek were now far behind her, running and tumbling down the mountainside.

She found her body where she left it, safely sleeping in the tree, and she entered in. The sudden weight of mortality was hard to get used to, but she quickly adjusted and made her way down the tree.

Everything came back to her in a rush. She recalled the reports of an approaching meteor, the falling objects depicted in the cave paintings, Xrys' belief that a sign from the heavens signaled the beginning of the end.

She wondered if her mom's hope that the government would destroy the meteor was what she just witnessed in the night sky.

Regardless of what just happened, she now was

faced with a decision. Should she try to find her mother, or make her way to the "Calendar," as Xrys had exhorted her to do? She was scared for her mother, and scared for herself, but she had to make a decision now and set her path, or she would soon be discovered by the retreating Lamek.

She recalled Xrys' simple faith. He had lived a life of mortal captivity, yet he still valued life.

His dedication to the Creator was unwavering, even when questions arose. But what struck her more deeply were his last few acts of selflessness. Despite the fact that he had had no time to store up energy, he had been walking alongside Kit to make sure she was safe, for Marai's sake. He had never told Marai that was his intention, but he had stayed with her mom, seeking no recognition, ultimately to his own detriment.

He believed so wholly in Marai, that she was now certain it was *he* who had been watching her and her mother huddling scared under a waterfall, and had exhorted Atl send back men to protect them. He spent his entire life watching for her and waiting. There were probably few moments since she had entered the rainforest that he had not dedicated his undivided attention to her cause.

It was humbling. He had given his life to save

hers, and then tried as best he could to save and comfort others.

What would it all come to if she didn't justify his faith in her? Marai removed her shoes and pack, and started walking downriver.

XVII

Marai walked through the next day and most of the night, passing by the lake and waterfall that marked the edge of Tutek territory early on. She let her feelings guide her as she walked, hoping to see something soon that resembled a calendar. She managed to avoid any Lamek villages, and took that as a sign that she was being guided.

When she decided to finally rest, Marai climbed a tree and watched the still-dark sky for any further signs of the meteor. Perhaps her mom had been right and everyone's worries were unfounded. It would be really unfortunate if millennia of end-times prophecy had been undone by modern technology, but if that was the case, she decided it was a good problem to have.

Just as she thought this, another light appeared in the sky up near the Sacred Mountain. This one was not as large as the first, nor as high, and it had tails following it like something entering the atmosphere. For some reason, Marai could not bring herself to take her eyes off the object. It soon stopped burning but she kept her eyes on its path as it fell, which was easier to do while the light of dawn appeared and the sky lightened. Perhaps it was a piece of debris from the meteor?

She watched for an hour or so. If this was how the world was going to end, she wanted to see it coming the whole way. The strange thing was, it almost looked like it was heading her way. Thirty minutes later, and she was convinced it was going to land on the continent.

A low rumble sounded in the sky as it came near. She clenched her eyes tightly and waited for the impact to take her to the other side. An enormous reverberation shook her to her core, and the only thing Marai could compare it to was the sonic boom of a fly-by she had witnessed at an air show when she was younger. She waited for death to take her, wondering what it would feel like.

Almost as soon as it started, it was gone. Marai opened her eyes and looked at her hands.

She was still in the tree, and she was not glowing as one deceased. Perhaps the object had landed far enough away that it spared her, even though she felt the shaking from it.

She wondered if more would follow. She set her jaw, climbed down the tree and began to travel again. If the world was going to end and they were all going to die, she might as well go out trying to fulfill a dead man's wish. What else was she going to do?

A strange thing happened while she traveled. Marai saw a parachute tangled in a tree, and she stopped to look around. It appeared as if someone had detached him or herself from the chute and had made his or her way to the river. The tracks were fresh enough that even *she* could follow them. She was following the tracks when she heard some noise up ahead. She looked up and saw a man dressed in what looked like a spacesuit, hunched down and taking a drink from a thick straw placed in the river. He startled and stood up when he heard her approach.

"Did they send you to bring me back?" he asked.

He spoke English. Was this the person she was supposed to meet?

"Is this the Calendar?" she asked. It didn't look different from any other piece of rainforest she had seen.

"What the heck are you talking about?" he said.

"I… I'm supposed to meet someone."

"Well if it's me, then lead the way," he said. "I'm not sure I'd like this place even if it is my only option! And why on Earth are they sending little girls to bring me back? We really could use a trained squad to find him out here!" She started to get a bad feeling.

Why on Earth…?

"I think I made a mistake," Marai said. She turned to leave.

"Wait, little girl!" he yelled, trying to limp after her.

"I'm sorry," she said. She started to run.

"Wait!" he yelled. "Wait, dad-gummit!"

Marai left him in her dust and started to open her mind once again. She needed to do less thinking and more feeling, letting her spirit guide her. Deep down, she felt that was not the meeting that was supposed to take place.

As it started to get dark, she felt the need to turn up a hill. She couldn't make out any details of where she was heading because of the trees surrounding her, but she got a feeling her destination was close by. The hill turned out to be a plateau clear of trees. In the middle of the clearing was a ring of tall rocks planted vertically in the ground. Some of them had stone lintels balanced across their tops. She realized that from the sky, it might look like a dotted circle, similar to the dotted circle in the cave drawing.

This felt like the right place.

She walked inside of the ring of rocks, wondering about its function. When she stood in the very center, it became apparent. Directly above one lintel, she could see the moon in the distance. Above other lintels, constellations, planets, and bright stars were perfectly aligned. This structure was built to mark a certain night; tonight.

The Calendar.

She heard a noise coming up the canyon, and ran to hide behind a stone. It was too far for her to run back to the trees.

To her amazement, what looked to her like a spaceship rounded a mountain and pulled up directly above the circular ring. The ship had bright lights illuminating the ground below it, and started to slowly descend.

Marai felt a twinge of excitement fill her breast, but she looked deeper and felt the warm confirmation that she was safe. She was doing the Creator's work. If not for her, then for Xrys.

Perhaps her rendezvous with this visitor would be salvation from the falling meteorites?

After all, the visitor had been described as "He-Who-Saves."

The ship landed softly on the ground in the center of the ring. She didn't know what to expect when the visitor emerged. She had her own ideas of what alien life looked like, and maybe the image depicted on the cave wall

indicated large eyes or something. Regardless of what he—
or it—looked like, she wanted to stay hidden until she saw
what she was dealing with.

A ramp lowered. What seemed like minutes passed
before a door opened. Out of the bright lights of the inside
of the spaceship, a figure emerged. It looked humanoid to
Marai, but she couldn't make out many details in its
silhouette. She found it hard to move out of hiding.

Trust me.

She heard the words as if they had been spoken
aloud. The Creator had a plan for her. She held onto that
faith which had sustained Xrys and had led her here, and
took a step out from behind the stone.

The figure stopped. It was unsure, too.

Marai took a few more steps toward the ship so it
could see she meant it no harm and get a better look at it.
She got close enough that she could make out some
features.

He was human!

The visitor was a boy about her age with dark hair
and piercing blue eyes. He smiled pleasantly at her. She
decided to speak to him.

"Hello," she said.